Cousins In Action
Operation Jewel Thief

Sam Boud

Cousins In Action

Operation Jewel Thief

**FOREST TRAIL LIBRARY
EANES ISD**

* * *

Sam Bond

Cover Art by
Han Randhawa

BOUND PUBLISHING / AUSTIN, TX

Bound Publishing
5cousinsinaction@gmail.com
www.5CousinsAdventures.com

Publisher's Note: This is a work of fiction. Names, characters, places, and incidents are a product of the author's imagination. Locales and public names are sometimes used for atmospheric purposes. Any resemblance to actual people, living or dead, or to businesses, companies, events, institutions, or locales is completely coincidental.

Book design © 2015, BookDesignTemplates.com

First Edition vs 1.

ISBN 978-0-9911914-5-1

[1. England – Fiction. 2. Mystery – Fiction. 3. Cousins – Fiction.

4. Adoption – Fiction. 5. Crown Jewels – Fiction. 6. Travel – Fiction.

7. Spy – Fiction 8. Adventure – Fiction]

Printed in the United States of America

For Sylvie, Angela, Helen,
Fiona and Sara-Jane
Five of my crazy English friends

"A mystery is a puzzle waiting to be solved."
Tess B-K

mystery [mist(ə)rē]

1. something that is difficult or impossible to understand or explain.

2. a novel, play or movie dealing with a puzzling crime, especially a murder.

1

Dead

Olivia let out a piercing scream and landed in a crumpled heap at the bottom of the live oak. "She's dead! DEAD, I tell you!" bellowed Tess, from beneath the study window.

Cagney smoothed down her shorts and leisurely crossed the lawn. Tess scrunched up her tutu and bounded after her. The two girls crouched over Olivia's lifeless body.

"Check her pulse," said Cagney, loudly.

"Is she breathing?" yelled Tess.

The two cousins checked the study window.

Olivia opened an eye. "Is she coming?"

"Not if you don't keep still, she won't," said Cagney.

"Maybe it would help if you moaned a bit," suggested Tess.

"I'm not moaning," said Olivia. "I'd feel stupid."

"I will," said Tess. "I'm used to feeling stupid."

Tess let out a moan that any self-respecting ghoul would be proud of.

Cagney clapped her hand over her cousin's mouth. "You're not helping."

"We should have used ketchup," said Olivia. "I told you, the only thing to get Grandma out of her study is blood. Lots of blood."

Cagney sighed. She'd rather eat grass than admit it, but Olivia was right.

Since the beginning of summer Grandma had become ever so slightly strange. To be honest, she'd never been normal, but after two back-to-back trips to Peru and India, Grandma had returned home to a phone that would not stop ringing and a study the cousins were no longer welcome in.

Locks had been placed on the study door, and Grandma never left the room without making sure they were all secure. The closet had been cleaned of clutter, and the cousins had a sneaky suspicion something else had taken its place – but what? All attempts at questioning were avoided, and even sweet little Lissy was having no joy in wheedling information from their normally talkative Grandma.

The cousins were determined to figure out what was going on and had hatched a plan – a plan that currently wasn't going too well.

There were five cousins in all, two born in China, three born in the U.S. Cagney, the oldest, was twelve; Tess, the youngest, six. Aidan, the only boy, came sandwiched in the middle. Lissy, Aidan and Cagney had fair hair and hazel eyes. Olivia and Tess, dark hair and even darker eyes. The one thing they had in common was their size – all five were the smallest in their grade, by a lot.

Tess produced another high-pitched scream.

"Will you stop doing that?" hissed Olivia. "This is a dumb plan. Grandma's never going to fall for …"

Cagney gasped. "The blinds moved."

"This is an awesome plan," said Olivia, sitting up.

"Be quiet!" Cagney shoved Olivia backwards. "You're supposed to be unconscious."

"Oh yeah!" Olivia flopped onto the yellow grass. "I forgot."

Grandma Callie shuffled out of her study. She shuffled into the kitchen and shuffled through the screen door, letting it slam sharply behind her.

This was exactly what Lissy and Aidan were waiting for.

2

Break In

Two pairs of hazel eyes emerged from the hall closet.

"Is it open?" whispered Lissy.

Aidan peered down the hall. "Houston, we have lift-off!"

Lissy and Aidan scooted towards Grandma Callie's study and slipped through the door. Silently, they gazed around the forbidden room. It was not a frivolous room. Plopped in the middle sat a sturdy wooden desk. It was bookended by two sets of drawers, a wooden chair on wheels lounging abandoned in the middle. Between two windows stood an overstuffed bookcase and, on a side table, a cage of snoozing rats.

The cousins scanned the room looking for one thing – the closet. Hidden behind the desk, Aidan spied a handle set into the wall and hurried towards it.

"Wait!" Lissy grabbed the back of Aidan's tee. He boomeranged back towards her. "What if it's got an alarm?"

Aidan gulped. "Too late to worry now. Just keep watch. Let me know if Grandma heads back to the house."

Lissy crossed the study, lifted a slat of the heavy blinds and peeked through. "It's okay. She's too busy yelling."

"Excellent. She could be there for hours – days, in fact. Now, if I could just get this stupid door open."

"I'm still not sure we should be doing this," Lissy murmured anxiously.

"I know. I feel bad, too. But how else are we going to find out what's in here?"

"We could just ask." Lissy plucked a photo frame off the book shelf.

"We've tried that." Aidan tugged the doorknob. "Grandma wiggles out of everything."

Lissy nodded. "Yep. She's good."

"Yeah," said Aidan. "Too good."

"There's Grandma," exclaimed Lissy.

"What?" Aidan's knees buckled.

"In these pictures," said Lissy. "Here's one of her at the Great Wall of China and another by the Eiffel Tower."

Aidan hurried over to the bookcase and examined the pictures. "Look at her here, skiing with four guys."

Lissy wrenched the frame out of Aidan's hands. "Those aren't guys. Those are our fathers."

Aidan peered closely at four men, a much younger Grandma, plus a young woman he did not recognize. Grinning broadly, the six stood at the top of a mountain, their poles pointed towards a black sign.

"You don't think they actually skied down that, do you?" asked Lissy. "Double black diamonds are really hard."

"Nah! Pa can't ski to save his life. What about your dad?"

"No way! Dad gets vertigo if he stands too fast. He couldn't make it down the bunny run."

Aidan shrugged. "Come on. Make sure Grandma's still dealing with Olivia while I look in the closet."

Lissy hoisted the blinds in time to see Grandma unceremoniously scoop Olivia up and dump her on her feet.

Aidan bolted back to the closet. He wiggled the latch – nothing. He prodded with his shoulder – nothing. Finally, he grasped the doorknob and pulled with all his strength – bingo! The door handle came off in his hand. "Oops!"

"Aidan! What have you done?"

Aidan glanced around sheepishly and hid the doorknob behind his back. "Nothing!"

"Give it to me."

Aidan shrugged. "I don't know what happened. It just came off."

Lissy shook her head. The word 'boys' came to mind, but she suppressed it. She liked Aidan. He was a great cousin, even if he *was* a boy. Carefully she replaced the door handle on its stick.

"Thanks," said Aidan. "But how else was I supposed to open it?"

"Keys," replied Lissy. "Did you look for a key?"

Aidan grimaced. "Not so much."

Lissy shimmied open Grandma's desk drawer and rummaged. She snatched up several passports and tossed them on the desk. "That's funny. Grandma has different passports."

"She has dual citizenship, remember? British passports look different to ours."

Lissy flipped the passports over. "Yes, but these passports aren't British *or* American."

"What?" Aidan picked up three passports and flicked through them. "These aren't Grandma's. They have different names."

"*She* looks familiar." Lissy jabbed a finger towards the green passport. "Kind of like a much younger Grandma, but with different hair, different colored eyes and whoa, look at that nose! Do you think they might be cousins or something?"

"Maybe," said Aidan. "Who do they belong to?"

"The Australian passport belongs to Caren Durrell, the South African to Naomi Muller and the Italian one says Magdalena Rossi."

Aidan scratched his head. "I've never heard of them. Do you think they're distant relations?"

"I don't know. But there's something very familiar about them." Lissy shoved the passports back into the desk drawer and pulled out her clasped fist. "Got it!" She opened her fingers and revealed a bunch of shiny copper keys.

Aidan grasped the keys and headed towards the closet. Ramming one of the keys in the lock, he jammed it to the right until he heard a soft click.

Aidan grinned. "First time lucky. What were the chances?"

"Quick, just look inside." Lissy pushed the desk drawer back and headed to the window.

Aidan turned the handle and pulled. The door gave a click and swung gently open.

"Oh no! They've gone!"

Aidan closed his eyes. "Who's gone?"

Lissy gulped in air. "Everyone!"

"Holy moly." Aidan slammed the door shut. "Then if Grandma's not in the garden, where is she?"

The telephone trilled.

Lissy's eyes bulged. "In the name of Great Aunt Maud! She's going to kill us."

Aidan didn't have time to agree as the answer machine clicked on.

"Callie! It's Max. There's been another one. We will arrange the usual, and Gilbert's on his way. Pack your suitcase, Callie. You're going to London."

The cousins stared at the phone. They stared at each other. Then they stared at the door, eyes widening at the terrifying sound of fluffy slippers shuffling towards it.

3

Trespassers

Aidan looked frantically around the room. "We've got to hide."

"Duh! But where?"

"Anywhere!" said Aidan, desperately.

The cousins spied the large wooden desk at the same time. Lissy yanked out the chair and crawled beneath. Aidan quickly followed, dragging the chair in behind them.

It took about two seconds for them to realize they were not alone, as a fat, indignant snake rose from its coils.

"Move over, Hiss." Lissy gave the boa constrictor a hefty push. "There's not room for three of us." Lissy tapped Aidan on the shoulder. "Could I get some help here, please?"

Aidan tore his eyes from the door and sighed. Grabbing the enormous snake under its belly, he helped Lissy hoist the reluctant reptile onto the wooden chair. True to his name, Hiss stuck out his tongue in displeasure. Lissy poked hers out in reply, but immediately her gaze caught on something else. Something copper dangled from the closet door. Lissy scrambled to her knees to get a better look.

"Lissy, get down!"

"Keys!" Lissy pointed towards the closet. "You left the keys in the lock."

Aidan gulped, but there was nothing he could do. Slowly, the door to the study opened and in shuffled a pair of fluffy slippers. Hidden by the large wooden desk, the cousins watched the slippers patter towards them.

Aidan's heart hammered. Thoughts of groundings for life and years of chores swirled through his mind. He shook his head. What was he thinking? That was the *good* scenario. Aidan broke into a sweat imagining the alternatives.

The slippers shuffled closer. Stopping by the side of the desk, Grandma Callie leaned over and hit play on the answer machine. Max repeated his message. *Just delaying the agony*, thought Aidan, as the slippers padded towards them.

Just when Aidan figured their lives were not worth living he heard a loud rat-a-tat-tat at the front door. Grandma's slippers paused, turned and shuffled back into the hallway.

Aidan thought he would faint. His pulse raced, his knees trembled and the taste of this morning's Coco Pops filled his mouth. Aidan swallowed hard. This was no time to lose his breakfast. There would be plenty of time for that later.

"Quick!" Lissy scampered out from their hiding place. Hurtling towards the closet door, she wrestled the keys from the lock and tossed them to Aidan, who promptly dropped them. Hand-eye coordination had never been his strong point. Aidan scooped up the keys and flung them into the desk drawer.

Lissy was already approaching the exit. Aidan was seconds behind. Lissy inched open the door and peeped through the crack. Grandma had stepped onto the front stoop and was talking to her neighbor, Mrs. Snoops.

In a flash, Aidan was off. Hurtling along the hallway, he crashed through their bedroom door and toppled to his knees. Lissy was close behind and managed an elegant somersault over her cousin's back before landing face down on the nearest bed.

The cousins' room was less of a bedroom - more of a bunkhouse. Five single beds lounged against the farthest wall and two wide windows, on either end, flooded the room with light.

Cagney leapt to her feet. "Well? What took so long?"

Lissy rolled her eyes. This was so like Cagney. Lissy made a mental vow: Next time anyone risked incurring the wrath of Grandma, it would *not* be her.

Aidan looked decidedly pale. His voice, when it came, was high and scratchy. "I don't think I can bear to talk about it yet."

Lissy grabbed her laptop, Spider, and flipped her open. "Remind me again, why *we* were chosen to break into the study?"

"Because you two are by far the most trustworthy, and Grandma would *never* suspect you getting up to no good," said Olivia, in a sing-song voice.

"Whereas, for some reason, we're a bit more suspect." Tess shoveled the last of a banana into her mouth and gave a mushy smile.

"Oh yeah!" Lissy fired up Spider. "I knew there was *some* reason."

Aidan focused on the bag of defrosting vegetables slumped on the bed next to Olivia. Vegetables Olivia had been instructed to apply to her forehead, her foot and a place she'd rather not mention. "Did Grandma believe you'd fallen out the live oak?"

"Oh these?" Olivia poked the half-frozen bag. "Debatable. I figured I'd hit the ground so many times before that she'd ignore me."

"But as soon as she started howling, Grandma came running," said Cagney.

"It was really more of a shuffle," corrected Tess.

"Let's get this straight," said Olivia. "I did *not* howl."

"You did when Tess head-butted you on the plane coming back from India," said Cagney.

Olivia grimaced. It was well known that her sister had the hardest head of any human - ever. Not only was it hard, but it seemed to be continually in motion, a potentially deadly combination.

"Well, it worked. We got in," said Lissy, tapping a few keys.

"Of course you got in. My master plans never fail," said Cagney.

"*Your* master plan?" said Olivia.

Lissy ignored her dueling cousins and told them about the message from London. When she got to the part about the passports, Olivia almost fell off the bed, causing half-thawed peas and carrots to careen across the carpet.

"Are you *sure* they were all different people?" asked Olivia.

"They had different names. Came from different countries. And they all looked similar, but definitely different," said Lissy.

Aidan frowned. "Why do you ask?"

"Because I have a theory," said Olivia.

"I also have a theory." Lissy turned Spider to face the others. "Look at this."

Filling Spider's screen with big bold letters were the words:

CROWN JEWELS – STOLEN

LONDON POLICE BAFFLED

"You don't think?" said Aidan.

"Oh yes I do," said Lissy. "Don't you?"

"Think what?" asked Tess.

"That Grandma flying to London right after the crown jewels go missing is not a coincidence," said Lissy.

"Oh!" Tess shook her head. "Course not."

"And one more thing." Lissy turned to Olivia. "Can your dad ski?"

"Ski?" Olivia looked puzzled. "Have you *seen* my dad?"

"Why?" asked Tess.

But before Lissy had a chance to tell the girls about the picture of their fathers, the door flew open revealing the most enormous man the cousins had ever seen. A man dressed all in black.

4

Man vs. Snake

The man's bulk filled the entire door frame. In one arm he held a cage full of rats, in the other, a cage full of Chaos. Hiss swarmed around his neck. Tess gave their grandma's pet sitter a pinky wave.

"Yo!" Sneezy strode into the room, instantly making it feel a lot smaller. "I'm looking for your grandma."

"Haven't seen her in hours," said Aidan, a little too quickly.

"Barely seen her in days," said Lissy, slipping Spider under her pillow.

"Hmm!" said Sneezy. "You don't look very surprised to see me."

"With Grandma off to London, we figured we'd see you soon," said Aidan.

Sneezy frowned. "How'd you know your grandma's off to London?"

"We … we … don't," stammered Aidan. "I mean… if you're here we've got to assume she's off somewhere, right?"

"And London's so wonderful at this time of year," said Lissy. "You know … all that rain."

Sneezy's dark eyes narrowed. "Anyhow, I just wanted to let your grandma know I came prepared." He rattled the cages proudly. "No climbing live oaks capturing uncooperative felines this time." Sneezy raised the cage containing Chaos to eye level and peered inside. A very annoyed ball of gray fluff peered back. Sneezy quickly lowered the cage. "No, siree. I have myself a well-executed plan."

"But what about Hiss?" asked Tess. "Where's Hiss' cage?"

"I figured I could keep Hiss right up here." Sneezy flexed his shoulders. "You know, until I get myself to head-quar …" The pet sitter stopped. "I mean, to the pet sitter place."

Aidan and Lissy exchanged glances.

"Around your neck?" Olivia sounded concerned. "You know, I've been thinking about that, and it's probably not a good idea to keep Hiss around your neck for any length of time."

"I'll ..." The pet sitter coughed. "Be ..." He coughed some more, "... fine," he squeaked.

"Are you okay?" asked Tess.

Sneezy tried to clear his throat. "Is it hot in here? It suddenly seems extremely hot in here."

"It's Texas," replied Cagney. "It's always hot."

"I'm starting to feel a little dizzy." The pet sitter began to sway.

"Cripes!" said Olivia. "It's Hiss. He's constricting!"

The five gawked in horror as Sneezy's dark face drained of color. He stiffened and, without warning, toppled like a tree trunk.

"Timber!" yelled Olivia, as Sneezy hit the floor nose first.

The large man bounced several times before coming to a stop.

"Rats!" screamed Cagney.

"I know, this is dreadful," said Lissy, rushing to Sneezy's side.

"No, I mean rats! Everywhere!" yelled Cagney.

Upon hitting the floor, the cage of rats had burst open and tiny feet were scampering in every direction. The other cage also lay empty. Lissy turned in time to see a fluffy gray tail disappear into the hallway with Hiss slithering boldly behind.

Cagney leapt onto the bed. "Nobody hit the manic button," she yelled. "The thing is not to manic!"

Olivia gazed quizzically at Aidan.

"She means panic," said Aidan, who was normally the one who could best translate his sister's muddles.

"I said *not* to panic," said Cagney, indignantly.

Aidan grinned at Olivia. "Told ya."

Tess stared at the large man. "I hope he's not dead. My pink fluffy tutu is not good with dead people."

Olivia dropped to the ground and unsuccessfully tried to roll Sneezy over. "I could do with some help here, guys."

Lissy, Tess and Aidan gathered around.

"On the count of three," ordered Cagney. "One, two ..."

The cousins gave an almighty heave. Sneezy didn't budge.

"Put your back into it," yelled Cagney.

Olivia gave her cousin a look.

"Let's try rocking him," said Lissy. "We need to gain momentum."

The cousins rocked the pet sitter back and forth until, with a dull thud, he tumbled onto his back.

The five stared at Sneezy's face. With eyes tight shut and mouth wide open, it was not Sneezy's most attractive look. It was not helped by the blood oozing from his teeth, nor the angle of his nose, which was wedged to the side and swelling magnificently.

Olivia watched a stray rat carrying a carrot between its teeth hurtle across the pet sitter's belly, before scurrying out the door.

Tess reached forward and tried to push Sneezy's nose back to where it belonged.

Sneezy's eyes blinked open. "Ger off be doze!"

"At least he's breathing," said Aidan, doing his best not to look at the blood.

Lissy shook her head. "I hate to say it, but when he sees his nose, he might wish he wasn't."

*
*
*
*

5

The Mystery of the English Language

Within two hours of Sneezy breaking his nose, Grandma was packed and heading down the garden path. The cousins watched a yellow Humvee round the corner, and, without a backward glance, Grandma climbed in and departed.

Mrs. Snoops was left in charge and had promptly taken the five shopping to buy waterproof jackets and something she insisted the English called 'wellies' - which turned out to be rubber boots. The cousins were to cross the Atlantic and join Grandma in London the next day. At least, that had been the plan.

The cousins careened through the airport. A combination of Mrs. Snoops driving, plus Tess having to pee - twice - had made them disastrously late.

"Cripes!" said Lissy. "Grandma will be furious if we miss the plane."

"Yeah." Olivia bounded along beside her. "I can just imagine her face when she arrives at Heathrow and we're not there. That would be just awful!"

Lissy shook her head. Sarcasm should have been Olivia's middle name, however Lissy was pretty sure her cousin's middle name was something Chinese and unpronounceable.

Cagney's breath was ragged. "Are you saying you *want* to miss this flight?"

Olivia peered over her shoulder. Her cousin was not having an easy time. With a humongous bag thrust around her neck and a suitcase roughly the size of a fridge wobbling behind her, Cagney was having difficulty keeping up. Olivia glanced at her compact carry-on and gave thanks she was a low-maintenance kind of traveler. "Miss the plane? Heck no."

Lissy checked her watch. "Then run."

*

✳

✳

Olivia peered out the oval window at the blue sky below. "At least you won't have to learn a different language for this trip, Aidan."

Aidan gulped down a couple of motion sickness tablets and checked the seat pocket for an airsick bag. Aidan was always ready for adventure but wished he didn't have to board a plane to reach it.

The cousins had been the last to board the plane and had been certain they were going to miss it. They would never know if the airline official held the plane for no apparent reason, or because she was transfixed by the sight of a small Chinese child hurtling towards the departure gate. A child, dressed from rain hat to wellies in pink and waving a luminous polka-dot umbrella. However, hold it she did.

"Yep, it will be great going to a country where people speak the same language," said Lissy, tugging Spider out of her bag.

"Actually, there's a saying: England and the United States – two countries divided by a common language," said Aidan, tightening his seatbelt.

Tess popped her head over the seat in front. "What does that mean?"

Aidan shrugged. "I'm not sure. But how bad can it be? It's English, right?"

The cousins were interrupted by the meal trolley rattling down the aisle.

"Hellooo," said the flight attendant in the strongest accent Tess had ever heard. Tess stared open-mouthed at a dark-haired woman.

"May I be helpin' yoo?"

Tess looked blanker still.

"Oh!" said Aidan, after several seconds. "She said, 'Can I help you'."

"That's right, laddy," said the air steward.

Tess frowned. "I don't mean to be rude, but what language are you speaking?"

"I'm speakin' English," said the air steward, smiling broadly.

Lissy closed Spider. "I take it back. We're doomed."

"Does everyone sound like you in England?" asked Olivia.

"Och no!" said the air steward. "Only if ya lucky enough to come from Glasgow."

"That's in Scotland, isn't it?" asked Aidan.

"Och aye!" she replied, grinning.

"What's the difference between England and Scotland?" asked Tess. "I mean, apart from the accent."

"Och! I don't be having the time, but generally, we're a lot nicer!"

"Don't be listening to a word she says." A pretty redhead with a full face of freckles came bustling towards them. "Bonnie will be telling you all sorts of nonsense. Won't you now, Bonnie?"

"Are you from Scotland too?" asked Tess.

"Ah, be going on with you! I'm from Belfast," said the redhead, placing a tray in front of Cagney.

Seeing the cousins' blank faces, she added, "Northern Ireland."

"Your accent is really pretty," said Lissy, shyly. "But to us it's really strong."

The redhead laughed. "Get away with you now. If you want to be hearing a strong accent, it's the Welsh you should be listening to." The redhead indicated a small blonde steward in the next aisle. "Morwenna makes Bonnie and me sound like the queen."

Aidan watched the flight attendants retreat along the aisle. "They're joking, right? I can barely understand a word they're saying."

"Maybe we need to rethink the language thing," said Olivia. "Although, there's got to be some English people we can understand, right?"

There was silence.

"Oh come on, there's got to be someone," said Aidan.

"Harry Potter!" exclaimed Olivia. "I'm pretty sure he's English."

"Yep, but what about Hagrid?" said Aidan. "Every time he comes on the screen you ask me to translate."

Olivia shrugged. "What about the crocodile guy?"

"Australian," said Lissy.

"Are you sure?" asked Olivia.

Lissy pushed a curl off her forehead. "Not entirely. But I don't think England is exactly known for its diverse crocodile population."

"There's always our dads," suggested Tess.

Olivia shook her head. "And there we have the obvious."

"James Bond!" Cagney folded back the cover of *Clamour* revealing a full-color spread of a handsome man in a tuxedo. "There's someone we can all understand."

"Talking of James Bond. What about Grandma?" said Olivia, lowering her voice.

Cagney sighed and held the picture against her heart. "Grandma's *way* too old to have a crush on James Bond. I mean, she's ancient."

"That's not what I meant," said Olivia. "It's just Grandma's so secretive. And all those passports."

"Yeah," said Lissy, looking up from Spider. "I've no idea what's going on there, but at least when we get to England we can try and figure out why grandma flew to London right after the crown jewels went missing."

"What does Spider say about England?" asked Aidan.

"Do tell," said Cagney, sniffing the food before her suspiciously. "I'm sure it's absolutely fascinating - not."

Fortunately, Lissy was sitting behind Cagney and could not see her face. Lissy liked nothing better than to share what she learned from Spider and needed very little encouragement to do so.

Lissy shifted in her seat and raised her voice so the three in front could hear. "Spider says Great Britain is located in Europe and London is the capital. Apparently Britain is roughly the size of Oregon."

"Wow!" said Aidan "We're going to a floating island the size of Oregon - far out!"

"Great Britain consists of Scotland, Wales, Northern Ireland and England, which is where we're going," continued Lissy. "England, by itself, is even smaller."

"How much smaller can it get?" asked Cagney, who, coming from Texas, considered Oregon almost non-existent.

"Alabama," said Lissy.

"Double wow!" said Aidan.

Lissy smiled and continued. "But Britain is probably most famous for—"

"Not sinking?" suggested Cagney.

Lissy sighed. "No! Its royalty."

Tess paused mid-bite. "What do you mean? Like princesses and stuff?"

"Bingo!" said Lissy.

"You're telling me Britain the Great has real life princesses roaming the streets?" asked Tess.

"Well, I don't know about the roaming part," said Lissy, "but close enough."

Tess almost choked. "That's so cool."

"And, of course, where you find princesses, you find castles," continued Lissy.

Tess started to hyperventilate. "Get out of here."

"No really." Lissy smiled. "Great Britain is full of palaces and castles."

"Oh wow!" said Tess "My pink snazzy raincoat is going to *love* England. I might even get to wear my pink diamond tiara."

Lissy shook her head. If it were anyone else she would think they were joking. However, with Tess, she wasn't so sure. "Finally, Britain is located in the very western part of Europe. And they use pounds."

"What are pounds?" asked Olivia.

"What they use for money. Pretty much the rest of Europe adopted the Euro, but Britain stuck with their queen money." Lissy smiled. "Tess, their money has pictures of the queen on it!"

Tess clasped her hands together. "It just gets better and better."

Nine hours later the cousins descended through the clouds and touched down at Europe's busiest airport. Droplets of water cascaded along the windows as the huge jet skidded to a crawl and found a gate.

"Our grandma should be meeting us at Arrivals," said Cagney, as Bonnie and Morwenna herded the cousins through immigration and customs.

Bonnie scanned her clipboard and frowned. "Your grandma's name is William K. Fletcher?"

"Not when she left Texas, it wasn't," said Olivia.

"Well," said Bonnie, "I'm sorry to tell you, but I've got instructions to hand you over to a Mr. W. K. Fletcher. I'm no expert, but, if he turns out to be your grandma, I tell you, it'll be a first."

*
*
*

6

Introducing Billy

Lissy clutched Spider and stared at Bonnie in disbelief. "Who on earth is W. K. Fletcher?"

"Did I 'ear me name?"

Lissy spun around in time to see a skinny young man, with pink spiky hair and way too many piercings emerge from the crowd. The youth was dressed from head to foot in black. Instead of a belt, a silver chain wound around his waist and a tee-shirt, with the logo of a band Lissy had never heard of, plastered his chest. His pants were skin-tight and a pair of biker boots traveled halfway to his knees. A studded leather jacket and a broad smile completed the outfit.

"Wow!" said Tess, reaching towards the strange looking man. "Look at that hair."

"Don't even think about it," said Olivia, holding her sister back.

"I bet he has a hard time getting through security," whispered Lissy, counting the number of piercings.

Cagney's mouth hung open. Aidan's wasn't far behind.

"But who *are* you?" asked Cagney, pulling herself together.

"Billy Fletcher at your service," said the man, grinning from ear to stud. Reaching into his back pocket, he tossed his ID to Bonnie, grabbed the clipboard and, with a flourish, signed on the dotted line.

"Let me take a gander," said Billy, squatting to inspect Cagney. "Pretty as a picture, hazel eyes and curls - you've got to be Cagney."

Cagney took a step back, but flushed pink, all the same.

"So, that must make you smart little Lissy Bird," said Billy, noticing Spider clasped in the young girl's arms.

Lissy managed to give Billy half a smile but clutched Spider a little tighter.

Billy turned to Tess, smiling at the child dressed entirely in pink.

"And I'm Tess," said Tess, instantly liking the friendly, albeit odd-looking man.

"'Course ya are." Billy straightened Tess' rain hat before turning to Olivia. "So you must be rough and tumble Olivia. Which only leaves Aidan. One poor bloke amongst this gaggle a girls! How dy'a put up wiv it, mate?"

"But who are *you?*" asked Cagney.

"I'ze Billy, ain't I."

"No! I mean *who* are you?" repeated Cagney.

"I'm a friend of Callie's," explained Billy.

"Of course you are," said Cagney, looking over the top of her glasses. "You look *exactly* like the type of person our grandma hangs with."

"Me and Callie go back years. Fick as fieves," said Billy, proudly.

Aidan leaned into Cagney's ear. "He means thick as—"

Cagney batted her brother away. "I know what he meant."

Bonnie smiled and handed Billy his ID. "Well, whoever you are, Mr. William Fletcher, they're all yours now."

Lissy viewed Bonnie incredulously. "You're leaving us with … with …" Lissy's parents had taught her that if she couldn't think of something nice to say she should say nothing. Lissy exhaled deeply and shut up.

Bonnie crouched down. "I'm sure he's not as bad as he looks."

Billy grinned. "A ringing endorsement, if ever I 'eard one. Brilliant! Come on then, let's get going. Jimmy'll be wondering where we got to."

Billy grabbed Cagney's suitcase and Tess' neon pink bag and, oblivious to the stares of fellow passengers, sauntered through Arrivals and into the morning mist.

Following Billy outside, Lissy shivered. The warmth of the terminal had been replaced by a dampness that seeped into her bones. It was hard to believe they were still in the same hemisphere -

summer in England was colder than Texas in December. "Are you taking us to Grandma?"

"Nah! We're going to the smoke," said Billy, removing his jacket and draping it around Lissy's shoulders. "Your grandma's gone outta town for a few days and I'ze got ya till tomorrow. Then I'm puttin' ya on the train up norf, like. You'll see your grandma then. All right?"

Cagney tapped Aidan on the shoulder. "Translation?"

Aidan shook his head, dumbfounded. "So Grandma's *not* in London?" Lissy scowled, as she shrugged into Billy's jacket, which was heavier than it looked and reached practically down to her knees.

"Nah, don't fink so."

"What's the smoke?" asked Tess.

Billy grinned. "It's London, innit?"

"Are we going on the underground?" asked Lissy, who had been studying the transportation system during the flight and was quite looking forward to hurtling around London on an underground train.

"We *could* ride the tube," said Billy, "but I personally prefer me Rolls."

"Okay." Cagney took a stand. "I am *completely* lost. What in goodness name are tubes and rolls? Are we talking about some kind of sandwich, here?"

Tess smacked her lips. "Oooh, I do hope so."

"The tube is the transportation system in London," said Lissy. "Its official name is the London Underground, but people call it the tube."

"Why?" asked Cagney.

Lissy shrugged. "Believe it or not, Cagney, I don't know everything."

Billy eyed Lissy. "You're a smart little muffin top, aren't you? Oy look, 'ere comes Jimmy now."

An impressive silver car glided through the haze and pulled up to the curb. An older man with a somber face and a peaked cap emerged from the driver's seat. Strolling to the sidewalk, he opened the rear door and stood at attention.

"Sir," he said with a nod to Aidan. "Madams," he added, with the emphasis on the 'mad' rather than the 'dams'.

Cagney snapped a picture of both Billy and the car. There was no way her friends would believe either of these apparitions unless she had documented proof.

Aidan scratched his head. "*This* is our ride?"

"Yep," said Billy, seizing Tess' neon pink suitcase and propelling it into the trunk. "Not bad, is it?"

"But this is a Rolls Royce." Olivia observed the two round headlights and the distinctive hood ornament in the shape of a woman diving into the rain. "It must have cost a fortune."

Billy grinned. "Just a small one. Jump in now, before Jimmy 'ere decides we ain't good enough."

Lissy checked the bottom of her shoes and, finding them clean, gingerly climbed in. The others clambered in behind her.

"That's the ticket," said Billy, sliding into the passenger seat.

Jimmy took his place behind the wheel and instantly the Rolls eased from the curb. The cousins were unusually quiet, and, other than Tess, who immediately drew a smiley face on the window, none of them touched anything.

Billy shifted in his seat. "'Ere! Relax. James knows what he's doing."

The Rolls sped out of the airport and sailed onto a wide street.

Cagney threw her hands over her eyes and squealed. "He's going to hit something."

Olivia squinted out the window. "Hit what?"

Cagney spread her fingers and peered through. "Anything that comes around that corner. Like that humongous, red, two story, aaargh, BUS!"

"That's called a double decker," said Lissy.

"I don't care what it's called," hissed Cagney. "He's on the wrong side of the road."

Lissy stifled a laugh, but Cagney saw it and glared at her cousin.

"It's not funny. Olivia said this car cost a fortune. I don't think it's going to be worth quite the same fortune if he hits something."

"Relax," said Lissy, in a most un-Lissy-like tone. "In England they drive on the left."

Cagney did not look convinced but continued to gape out the window, visibly wincing every time a car shot by.

"Mr. Fletcher?" said Lissy.

"Call me Billy."

"Well ... Mr. ... erm ... Billy," said Lissy. "Where are we going?"

"Oh yeah. Mum says I'd forget me own barnet if it wasn't screwed on tight, like."

"What's a barnet?" asked Tess, who was enjoying listening to Billy's strange way of saying things.

"It's yer 'ead, innit," said Billy. "Don't you lot speak English?"

"I think we learned several hours ago we don't," said Aidan. "We definitely speak American."

"Sir, where are you taking us?" asked Lissy.

"Oh yeah. We're off to the Featherington-Twits," said Billy.

Olivia frowned. "The Feathery whats?"

"Their London digs," said Billy. "Their main house is up norf, like, but they have a little flat we can use while they're in the country."

Olivia looked blank. "Whose London dig and what's flat?"

"Aidan, you're really going to have to learn this language," said Cagney. "This is worse than Peru *or* India."

"What I'm trying to say," said Billy, good naturedly, "is that I work for the Featherington-Twits. They're friends of your grandma's, and they asked me to make sure you didn't come to any harm, like. So, while you're in London, me and Jimmy 'ere's gonna look after you, ain't we, James?"

James' left eyebrow shot skyward.

Olivia wondered what 'Jimmy' thought of this plan. By the look of it, he wasn't too pleased.

"It's a pleasure, init?" Billy punched the chauffeur playfully on the arm.

This time both of James' eyebrows disappeared under his cap.

"I don't think he likes us," whispered Lissy.

"Who, old James 'ere? Jimmy loves everyone, don't you, Jim? He's just too bleedin' posh to show it!"

"Mister James?" Tess leaned forward in her seat. "Where are you taking us?"

"I am entirely at your service, madam. Your grandmother has asked me to take you wherever you want. Within reason," he added quickly.

"Excellent," said Cagney. "Being chauffeur-driven around London, what more could madam want?"

"And where, exactly, would madam like to go?" asked Olivia.

"Madam would like to go ..." Cagney stopped. "I don't know. Lissy, where *would* madam like to go?"

Lissy had already pulled out Spider and was busy tapping away. "Definitely the Tower." She gave Aidan a knowing look. "Then the Eye, St. Paul's, Westminster Cathedral ..."

"Yeah! What she said," said Cagney, cutting off her cousin as she settled back into the soft leather upholstery.

"Hey, wait a minute, you lot. We've only got one day 'ere; not a bleedin' fortnight."

Cagney gave Lissy a puzzled look. "Fortnight?"

Lissy smiled, this is why she loved research. "It's the way the British say 'two weeks'."

"Tomorrow you're bein' packed off to the country, like," Billy continued.

"We are?" Olivia whispered to Aidan. "How are we going to find out what Grandma's up to if we're only here for one day?"

Aidan leaned towards Billy. "Well, we definitely want to visit the Tower. The rest is optional."

"Let me see 'bout that. Could be a bit tricky what wiv the current situation." Billy fished a battered cell phone out of his pocket and punched in a number.

"He must mean the situation Grandma's dealing with," whispered Aidan.

"What have the missing jewels got to do with the Tower?" asked Tess.

"It's where they're kept. Or where they *were* kept until someone stole them," replied Lissy.

"Yeah," said Olivia. "If we have any hope of figuring out what Grandma's up to, then we've got to get to the Tower."

"It better not be a high tower," said Cagney, wincing as another double decker bus zoomed by. "I don't do heights."

"Ere, it's me, Billy - howzabout a tour, today? Friends of the Featherington-Twits ... Great. Fanks a bunch, me old pot." Billy stuffed his cell phone into his jacket pocket. "We're on! To the chopping block, Jimmy, me old mate."

7

London Town

James expertly maneuvered the Rolls through the London traffic, and despite Cagney gasping every time a car passed, they soon arrived in central London.

"Wow! What's that?" Olivia pointed at a round structure arching into the sky like a giant Ferris wheel.

"That's the London Eye," said Lissy. "On a clear day you can see for twenty-five miles. And over there's the Palace of Westminster. Better known as the Houses of Parliament. That's where the government works. It's kind of like our capitol."

Aidan studied the ornate cream building perched on the banks of the river.

Billy swiveled around. "Almost blown up, it was, back in 1605. Man named Guy Fawkes nearly got away wiv it too. On November 5th each year we celebrate by burning a 'guy' on top of a bonfire."

Cagney scowled. "Are you celebrating it *not* getting blown up, or that someone was trying?"

Billy frowned. "I don't rightly know."

"And that's St. Stephen's Tower." Lissy pointed at the famous clock tower sticking up from one end of the Houses of Parliament.

"No it's not," said Olivia. "That's Big Ben."

"Yeah, we saw it in Peter Pan, right Olivia?" agreed Tess.

"Big Ben is the bell *inside* the clock tower," said Lissy. "The tower itself is called St. Stephen's. It's a common mistake."

"Cor, she's a bleedin' know-it-all, ain't she?" Billy gave Lissy a wink. "You should start a tour, luv."

Lissy smiled shyly, not sure if this was a compliment. And definitely not sure if she liked being called 'luv'.

James swung the car onto a low bridge.

"This 'ere's the Thames," said Billy. "Runs right froo London."

"Is this the way to the Tower?" asked Lissy.

"We are making a slight detour to the Palace first, madam," replied James, nodding his head towards the clock tower.

Billy smiled. "Brilliant idea, Jimmy. We're gonna be just in time."

"There's a palace?" Tess bounced up and down. "Oooh! I *love* palaces."

"Have you ever *seen* a palace?" asked Cagney.

"Yes," said Tess, pointing towards the Palace of Westminster. "That one! But my pink flowery wellies say this one's going to be even *more* fabulous."

Billy stared at Tess. The others were used to Tess' clothing talking to her. It was easy to forget how weird it may seem to strangers. Billy ran his finger and thumb down his long pierced nose. "And I fawt I was crazy."

A few twists and turns later and the Rolls pulled onto a large boulevard.

"And here we have The Royal Mall," said James.

"They have a royal shopping mall?" Cagney lurched forward and peered out the window. "Is it just for royals, or can anyone shop there?"

Billy hid his smile behind his ringed fingers. "Nah, darlin'! Not *that* kind of mall. It's more like a kind a road, innit?"

Cagney slumped into her seat. "I knew it was too good to be true."

"Of course you did, madam," replied James.

Aidan grinned; it was fun seeing Cagney get a taste of her own sarcasm. James did deadpan like no one he'd ever met. Aidan began to think James had more of a sense of humor than he let on.

The Rolls Royce sailed up a wide avenue ablaze with flags, before circling around a large golden statue and gliding to a stop.

"Her majesty's London residence," pronounced James, with a hint of pride.

The cousins piled out of the Rolls and gazed at a large rectangular building that blended perfectly with the gray sky beyond. Tess wasn't sure if this was what she expected the home of a queen to look like. Where were the turrets? Where was the drawbridge? The only hint of color the building possessed was a flag with a harp and a dragon, fluttering merrily in the breeze. It didn't help that the palace was surrounded by a black iron fence, partially hidden by hundreds of tourists.

"What are they doing?" asked Cagney.

"You'll soon find out," replied Billy. "'Ere, follow me."

Aidan grabbed Tess' hand and started to edge through the spectators.

"Mind the 'air now, missus," said Billy, with affable confidence, his pink spiky hair narrowly missing a black and white polka-dot umbrella.

In seconds Billy reached the railings and showed the cousins a first-rate view of an empty courtyard.

"We all 'ere?" asked Billy, turning to count heads. "Wait, we're missing one!" Billy counted heads again. "Two dark, two blonde. Hmm, where's the annoying one?"

Aidan spun around. "Cagney!"

"I'm stuck," replied a terse voice.

"Oy you!" Billy pointed at a presumed German tourist with a camera in his hands and lederhosen on his legs. "'Ave an 'eart, will ya? Let the little girl frew."

Silently the tourist raised his camera and snapped a picture of Billy and his pink, spiky hair. Billy gave him a wink, and seconds later Cagney squeezed into view. Cagney gave Billy a murderous look. Billy ignored it. "Try to keep up next time, luv."

"Is this the queen's home?" asked Tess, bouncing up and down and sideways with excitement. "Is she home?"

"Sure is, sweet 'eart. See that flag, there?" Billy pointed a ringed finger towards a red yellow and blue flag. "That there's the Royal Standard. Always flies if the queen's in residence."

"I thought the Union Jack was the British flag," said Lissy. "You know, those red white and blue flags we saw coming up the mall."

"Right again," said Billy. "The Royal Standard is just used by the queen. Nice perk! Goes with the job."

Tess made a mental note to design her own flag as soon as she got home to Texas.

"So what *is* this place?" asked Cagney.

"This 'ere's Buckingham Palace, named, as one might suspect, after the Duke of Buckingham."

Olivia grinned. Billy was starting to grow on her.

Billy cleared his throat and waved his arm dramatically towards the Palace. "Built in seventeen-oh-free, it has been the official London residence of the king or queen since Vicky, who, if you should take a ganders, is sitting over there on her frone, like." Billy waved in the opposite direction towards a large winged statue, knocking the hat off the tourist to his right.

Billy scooped to pick up the hat and almost impaled the man. "Sorry 'bout that, mate."

The man grabbed his hat and took a hasty step back.

Billy continued. "BP, as we locals like to call it, comprises of 77,000 square feet and has the largest private garden in the 'ole of London. During World War Two the good old palace 'ere was bombed six times."

"Seven," said the hatless tourist.

Billy regarded him, quizzically. The man flapped a guidebook in Billy's face. Billy cleared his throat.

"During World War Two, the palace 'ere, was bombed *seven* times."

Cagney yawned. "So? Why are we here?"

"Any minute now, luv, and all will be revealed."

As if on cue the crowd broke into applause and, to Tess' delight, the courtyard started to fill with military men dressed in cherry red tunics and tall furry hats. Some held flags, some marched with guns, but the majority carried musical instruments, and were playing them enthusiastically.

"What are they doing?" asked Aidan.

"Oooh! I know." Tess craned her neck through the bars to get a better view. "It's the changing of the guard at Buckingham Palace. I know the song. *They're changing guards at Buckingham Palace ... Christopher Robin went down with Alice.*" Tess sung boisterously and out of tune.

"That's right, luv. Eleven-firty on the dot, rain or shine 'er majesty's guards put on a bit of a show, like."

"Will we see the queen?" asked Tess, scanning the courtyard. "Oh *please* tell me we're going to see the queen. Does she play the tuba? The trombone? Ooooh, the drums?"

"She's in residence, luv, but I don't fink we're gonna see 'er today," said Billy.

Tess' shoulders drooped. "Ah, fooey!"

Thirty minutes later, the Royal Guards marched out of the palace grounds and the show was over. Within seconds the crowd dispersed and Billy led the cousins back towards the traffic circle. The Rolls was easy to spot as it swept to a halt. Billy counted the cousins into the car and stopped when he got to four. "All right, who we missing now?"

"Well, it's not me this time," said Cagney, sliding across the leather seat.

"It's Tess!" cried Lissy, pointing towards the Palace.

Everyone turned and, sure enough, Tess still clung to the bars.

"I'll get her!" Olivia sprinted towards her sister. "Tess, come on, you're not going to see the queen."

Tess did not move.

Olivia drew closer. "Tess, stop messing about. Come on. James is waiting."

Tess still didn't move.

"Do *not* make me come over and drag you," Olivia seethed.

Above the crowds and traffic Olivia heard a familiar sound. It was Tess, and she was crying. Olivia charged towards her sister, reaching the railings in seconds flat. Slapping her hand against her forehead, Olivia stared in horror.

8

Stuck

She's stuck!" explained Billy.

"I can see that," said the policeman. "Well and truly stuck."

In Tess' excitement she had leaned too far through the railings. Unfortunately, when it came time to lean back, her ears were in the way.

"Well, ain't you gonna get her out?" said Billy. "I mean we can 'ardly leave her 'ere, can we? And I don't fink her 'ead's gonna shrink."

Tess' hands started to flap. "Leave me? Olivia, don't let them leave me."

Olivia rolled her eyes.

Lissy stroked Tess' luminous pink raincoat. "Of course we're not going to let them leave you. I'm sure Billy has a plan." Lissy turned and glared at Billy. "You *do* have a plan, right?"

Billy winced. By this time a crowd had gathered, and Billy wasn't acting quite as confidently any more.

"I say we grab her legs and pull," said Olivia.

Tess scuttled her wellies away from the general direction of Olivia's voice.

"I mean, what's a couple of ears between sisters," said Olivia, grinning.

"Olivia!" said Lissy. "You can't be serious."

Cagney returned from the car with her camera. "Smile!"

Olivia, Aidan, Billy and the policeman gathered around Tess' protruding pink raincoat and struck a pose.

Lissy planted her hands on her hips and gave the policeman a withering look.

Catching her eye, the policeman drew back and cleared his throat. "Right then. Well, this isn't going to do, is it?"

"What do you *normally* do?" asked Aidan. "I mean, surely this can't be the first time someone got their head stuck?"

The policeman rubbed his chin. "Actually, I think it is."

"I believe *this* might help." The cousins turned to see James, a tub of Vaseline between his thumb and forefinger.

"Cor Blimey," said Billy. "The man in the cap has done it again."

Olivia grabbed the Vaseline from James' hand and flipped off the cap. She scooped out a large blob of Vaseline and, reaching forward, smeared it all over the sides of Tess' face.

"It's cold!" complained Tess.

"Ah, put a cork in it," said Cagney. "You want to stare at a gray building for the rest of your life?"

"Depends if I get to see the queen or not."

"The way this crowd is growing I'm surprised she's not come down herself," said Aidan.

Olivia examined her greasy fingers before seizing the bottom of Aidan's shirt and wiping her hands.

"Now pull," said Lissy. "Come on, Tess, you can do it."

Tess grabbed the railings. She plonked her flowery pink wellies against the low stone wall and pushed herself backwards.

Billy grabbed her around the waist and started to pull. Lissy wrapped her arms around Billy and tried to help. Aidan joined in and Tess squealed so loudly Aidan feared they really would see the queen, or at least a couple more policemen.

"It's funny you were talking about Christopher Robin," said Olivia. "Doesn't this remind everyone of when Pooh Bear got stuck in the—"

"You could help you know," said Lissy, scowling.

"Oh, alright." Olivia placed her arms around Aidan's waist and started to tug.

Cagney stared at James.

He shook his head. "Not in my job description, madam."

Cagney rolled her eyes as far back as they'd go before reluctantly wrapping her arms around Olivia's waist. Doing her best to ignore the tourist who was videoing them, she gave an almighty heave.

Without warning, Tess' ears gave way causing everyone to stagger back like dominoes. Cagney was the first to plummet to the ground. Olivia landed on top of her, and so the pile fell. Tess lay sprawled on top, rubbing her greasy ears.

"That wasn't too bad, was it?" said Billy, hoisting Tess and Lissy to their feet.

"Bad?" came Cagney's muffled squeak. "You think this isn't bad?"

Olivia wriggled out from underneath Aidan and pulled him upright. The only one left horizontal was Cagney, who lay flat on her back, floundering in a puddle.

Lissy sprung forward and helped Cagney to her feet.

"My pants!" exclaimed Cagney, inspecting her previously snow white jeans. "Are they ruined?"

"Barely," said Lissy. "Hardly at all."

"Couple of gallons of bleach and they'll be good as new," added Olivia, smothering her dimple.

"All right!" said Billy, shooing away the crowd. "Show's over."

The five clambered into the back of the Rolls and James steered the car away from the snapping tourists.

The Rolls took a sharp right and headed once more across the Thames.

"Jimmy's taking the scenic route," explained Billy.

Ten minutes later, Tess gave a squeal. "Oh look! It's London Bridge."

The Rolls was approaching the most unusual bridge Tess had ever seen. Two impressive blue towers rose at either end, with narrow walkways connecting them high above. James pulled up to one of the towers and stopped.

"Oooh, you're in for a treat now," said Billy.

"Why've we stopped?" asked Tess.

"We are making way for the H.M.S Lancashire," said James.

"Who the heck is the H.M.S. Lancashire?" asked Cagney.

"Her Majesty's ship, madam," replied James.

"Just you wait," said Billy.

The cousins watched in astonishment as the bridge split in two and started to rise.

"Holy moly," said Tess. "I've only ever seen small bridges do that, not a humongous bridge like this one."

"Yeah, it's wicked, innit?" said Billy. "Although, I gotta tell you, it's not London Bridge, it's Tower Bridge."

"Oh," said Tess. "Sorry."

"Don't you worry, luv. It's a common mistake. 'Appens all the time."

Once the bridge was flat, James glided over the magnificent structure and hung a left. A minute later the Rolls pulled up beside a stone castle.

"Her Majesty's Royal Palace and Fortress. Or, as it is more commonly referred to, The Tower of London," said James, formally.

Billy arranged a pickup time with James and, the logistics taken care of, everyone scrambled out of the Rolls. They scanned the fortress in front of them. A wide grass ditch surrounded it and sturdy stone walls stretched in either direction.

"It's like a castle," said Aidan.

"Where's the tower?" asked Tess.

"Well, it ain't like a tower these days. But back in the day, this fing 'ere would 'ave been the tallest building for miles. Come on. This way." Billy beckoned the five towards a side gate.

"Don't we have to buy tickets?" asked Lissy.

"Nah, not today. It's a bit shut right now."

"Why's it shut?" asked Tess.

"Yeah, well. Dunno if you 'eard, like, but there was a bit of a break-in a few days ago."

Lissy tried to hide her excitement. "Really? A break in? I *may* have done some light reading about it. Spider said it was the largest jewel heist ever. The thieves got away with several important pieces and the police are baffled."

"You got that right, luv. Come on. Let's get outta sight before the Old Nick sees us."

"The old what?" asked Aidan.

Billy jabbed his pink spiky hair in the direction of a policeman. "Coppers, policeman plod, you know."

Aidan shook his head. He really would have to start learning English and the sooner the better.

The cousins followed Billy towards a small door set into the wall.

"I called in a bit of a favor," said Billy, rapping the door three times and then twice more.

The door flung open and there stood an imposing man dressed in the weirdest outfit the cousins had ever seen. But it wasn't the outfit the cousins stared at. What they stared at was the incredibly sharp and deadly looking spear pointed right at them.

*
*
*

9

The Tower

issy shrieked.

"Keep it down, sweetheart," said the man with the spear. "Don't want the whole of London to hear ya."

The man towered above Billy, magnificent in an intricately embroidered red dress, with a large white ruffle around his neck. On his head perched a black hat with red, white and blue rosettes. Completing the ensemble were several medals, red stockings and something Lissy was pretty sure was called a garter.

The guy in the dress broke into an easy smile as he pulled Billy towards him. "Hello, son."

Lissy's jaw dropped.

Cagney's eyes became saucers. "That's your … this is your …" her eyes flicked back and forth between the two men. "No way!"

"Watchya mean? You can't see the family resemblance?" Billy patted the large man on the back. "Fanks, Dad. I owe ya."

Billy ushered the cousins through the door. Instantly the hustle and bustle of London traffic disappeared. The thick stone walls now had a more relevant use - they acted as sound proofing.

"Just the highlights if you don't mind, Dad."

"Rightcha, son." Billy's dad turned to the cousins. "Hello, little Americans. My name is Kevin. I will be your tour guide and would like to welcome you to one of London's most historic landmarks and my home."

The cousins followed Kevin along a narrow passage. Rounding a corner they came to a halt. The passageway opened onto a large courtyard, in the middle of which stood a light gray tower, three or four stories high. To the left sat a church and to the right, several narrow row houses. Kevin placed the dull end of his spear on the ground and cleared his throat.

"The Tower of London was built roughly nine-hundred years ago. It has been a prison, a planetarium and a bank, but what, pray, is it most famous for?"

"Ooooh! Ooooh!" Tess raised her hand. "I know this. No, I really do."

"We recognize the strawberry milkshake in the front here," said Kevin, indicating Tess.

Tess stepped forward, proudly. "Chopping people's heads off."

Kevin broke into a guffaw. "Well, I was gonna say the home of the crown jewels. But yes, sweetheart, several people met their demise within these walls. Queens such as Anne Boleyn and Katherine Howard, two of Henry the Eighth's more ill-fated wives; plus sixteen-year-old Lady Jane Grey met her death right here." Kevin picked up the spear and thumped it on the ground.

Lissy jumped.

"As you can imagine, The Tower of London is one of the most haunted sites in all England."

"What?" said Olivia. "You mean like ghosts?"

Kevin lowered his voice. "What I mean is, everyone and their Uncle Bob has a ghost story in a land this old. But this place is special. Many a young Yeoman's heart beats a little faster when he hears the sobs of Lady Jane Grey's husband at night. Not to mention when passing the White Tower and he sees the ghost of Lady Jane herself."

Lissy gulped.

"What's a Yeoman?" asked Tess.

"That would be moi, me little sugar plum fairy," said Kevin, bending to meet Tess' eye. "I am what you call the official bodyguard to the queen."

"They're also known as Beefeaters," said Billy, cheekily. "But Yeoman Warder's the official term."

"Of course this wasn't a regular prison," continued Kevin. "Only people of high status or treason were brought here. Guy Fawkes was hung, drawn and quartered after trying to blow up the Houses of Parliament."

"Billy told us about him earlier," said Lissy.

"Did he also tell you that before the state opening of parliament each year, we have to search the basement, just to make sure it's safe?" Kevin shook his head. "Four-hundred years later, and we still have to check for gunpowder."

Kevin ruffled the top of Olivia's short hair. "Here, we still got a few minutes before—. Well, what I'm trying to say is, we got a visitor coming. And it's probably best you lot are tucked away before they arrive."

Billy raised his eyebrows. "So that's why you're in full dress uniform."

"Aaah! You picked up on that did you, son? Yep, be here any minute. We better be quick, like. Come on, we'll just have a peek at Traitor's Gate."

"What about the crown jewels?" asked Lissy.

"Not today, sweetheart. It's a bit sensitive right now. We'll just have a quick look at Traitor's and then I got someone waiting to meet you back at the house." Kevin indicated one of the row houses. "A bit of royalty for you, East End style."

Lissy was disappointed, but what could she do? She couldn't force Kevin to take them to see where the jewels had been. Besides, what good would that do? They were gone. What was she expecting - a clue?

Kevin strode across the courtyard, leaving the cousins and Billy to follow.

"Cute birds." Tess waved her umbrella towards several black birds perched on a patch of emerald grass.

"Ravens have been living at the tower for over four-hundred years. Legend has it, if they ever leave the monarchy will crumble," said Kevin.

"No way! But what if they decide to make a break for it?" asked Tess.

Kevin whispered in Tess' ear. "I'll tell you a secret - they can't fly. They've got their wings clipped. Wouldn't even be able to make it to the top of the White Tower."

"Oh," said Tess. "That's sad."

Two minutes later the cousins arrived at a wooden gate set low in the thick stone wall. Beyond it, Olivia could see the shimmer of the Thames. Olivia realized it had stopped drizzling, and a beam of sunlight danced upon the river. Olivia thought of the wide blue Texas sky and wondered how people survived here with all this gray.

"This here is Traitor's Gate. The reason why it backs onto the River Thames is because the main way of getting about in Henry's time was by boat," said Kevin.

"Who is this Henry guy?" asked Cagney.

"King Henry the Eighth? He's about the most famous of all our kings. Mainly coz the silly bath bun took six wives," said Kevin.

"Six?" exclaimed Tess.

"Bath bun?" questioned Aidan.

"Don't you have rules about that kind of stuff?" asked Lissy.

"He didn't take 'em all at the same time," explained Kevin. "But six he took. Anyway, he was around in the sixteenth century, about five-hundred years ago, and when you were sent to the Tower you'd come through this gate here. Hence the name Traitor's Gate. This was often the last thing you saw of the outside world before your head was ..." Kevin broke off. "Well, before you died."

Lissy clutched her neck and gulped.

Kevin gave Lissy's hand a squeeze. "What you need is a nice cuppa tea, luv. Come on, I've got just the thing."

Lissy squinted up at the large man. "Sir, do they know how the crown jewels were stolen?"

"No, sweetheart. Nobody does. It's a mystery it is, good and proper. Got one of the best security systems in the world and still they managed to get away with some real nice stuff."

"What kind of stuff?" asked Cagney.

Kevin tapped the side of his nose. "Got to keep it on the QT, I'm afraid."

"But do the police have any suspects?" asked Lissy.

Kevin blew out a long breath. "I wish I knew."

"Do you know if the police have anyone helping them with their inquiries?" asked Aidan. "Maybe you've seen someone older hanging around the courtyard?"

"Yeah," said Tess. "Someone old and gray and probably wearing fluffy slippers."

Kevin's eyebrows raised. "Nope, no one of that description. Although I'll be sure to keep an eye out for the fluffy slippers."

A few minutes later the cousins arrived outside the old-fashioned row houses.

Kevin glanced at his watch. "Cripes, is that the time? I gotta get going. Our visitor should be arriving any second."

Kevin slapped Billy affectionately on the back before turning and heading towards the White Tower.

Billy rapped his knuckles on the door. "All right, you lot, let's go in and 'ave a cuppa."

"But where's Tess?" asked Lissy.

Billy spun one-hundred-and-eighty degrees. "Oh no! Not again." He clapped his hand to his forehead. "Dad's gonna kill me."

"She can't be too far. Let's go look for her." Olivia whirled around. Whereas before the courtyard had been empty, it was now packed with policemen.

Cagney snapped a picture. "What are they doing here? Don't tell me something else has gone missing?"

Billy trawled his fingers through the sides of his pink hair and sighed. "I think it means their special guest just arrived."

10

Royalty

illy went pale. "This is not cool."

"What's not cool, lad?"

Cagney spun around. In the doorway stood the third most peculiar person she'd seen that day. On any normal day the man before her would definitely have ranked in the top two, but this was far from a normal day.

Cagney raised her camera and snapped a picture. The slim, elderly man tipped his cap and smiled. He was dressed in a suit. However, the suit was not a regular black suit. In fact, Cagney had never seen a suit like it, as hundreds of tiny pearls sewn onto the fabric glistened in the fleeting sunshine.

Billy continued to scan the courtyard. "I've lost one of 'em, Grandad."

The man chuckled. "Well, Billy, you better go find 'em. I'll take your friends in for a cuppa, shall I? Hurry up now, your nan's waiting to see you."

"Are you Billy's grandpa?" asked Lissy.

"That I am, me luv. Name's Grandad Tom."

Tom shepherded the four into a pretty sitting room.

"Is that you, Billy?" A small, plump woman holding a tea tray bustled into the room. She was dressed in a similar outfit to Tom's, her skirt long and her jacket snugly fitted. She reminded Lissy of an elaborately decorated barrel.

"What do we have 'ere then?" The old lady's face broke into a wrinkled smile.

"These 'ere are Billy's friends from America, Iris. Kids, this 'ere is Iris, Billy's nan."

Iris placed the tea tray on a sideboard, grabbed a cup and saucer and thrust it into Olivia's hands. "A bunch of wooden planks, 'ere at Kev's. Who'd of thunk it?"

"Wooden what?" asked Cagney, grasping the cup of warm tea being offered.

"Wooden plank, Tom Hanks or, me personal favorite, septic tank." Iris finished giving out the teacups and eased into the largest of the armchairs. Her cheery face broke into a smile. "That's what you lot are called, innit?"

"Is it?" asked Lissy.

"What Iris is trying to say is, you're Yanks, aren't you?" said Tom, handing around a large plate of cookies.

Aidan grinned. "I guess so. We're from Texas."

"Ya see. That's what I was saying." Iris picked up a chocolate cookie and dipped it into her tea. "Come on now, don't be shy. Dunk your biscuits. It's the only way to eat 'em."

Lissy dipped the cookie into the brown liquid and popped it into her mouth. It melted instantly.

Following her cousin's lead, Cagney did the same. Her biscuit snapped in two and floated to the bottom of the cup. Cagney growled.

Tom placed the plate of cookies on a side table and settled himself into an armchair. "Iris is what they call a true Cockney."

"A cock-what?" asked Cagney, trying to figure out how to retrieve the cookie without using her fingers.

"Cockney. Born within the sound of Bow Bells," said Tom.

Cagney stared at Tom blankly.

Tom shifted forward and placed his teacup on his knee. "Let me explain. Iris and me were born in the East End. An area of London you might describe as working class. Anyhow, I'm an Eastender, born in Shoreditch, but Iris was born in Cheapside; just a few doors down from the church of Saint Mary-Le-Bow. So Iris 'ere's a Cockney. Coz, to be a true Cockney you 'ave to be born within the sound of Bow Bells."

"They were ringing as I popped into this world," said Iris, proudly. "Not many people can say that these days."

"But ma'am, why are you calling us a ..." Lissy cleared her throat. "A septic tank?"

"Coz she's speaking Cockney rhyming slang, ain't she? Tank rhymes with Yank, so therefore we call you a septic," explained Tom.

"But what's with the ... the ...?" Lissy motioned towards Iris' flamboyant outfit.

"You admiring me suit, luv? Tom and I are Shoreditch's pearly king and queen."

"Do you have to wear it all the time?" asked Lissy.

"Nah! Just on special occasions. Tom and I were appearing at a festival earlier today. We just stopped by to see our Kev on the way home."

Lissy shook her head. "I wish Tess was here. She's been wanting to meet a queen all day."

Iris eased herself out of her chair and spun slowly. She pointed to the various pearl shapes dotted all over her black suit. "See the different designs? They all mean different things. The horseshoe means good luck, of course. The heart means charity, and this pack of cards means life's a gamble."

"That's fascinating," said Lissy.

"But what does it mean?" asked Aidan. "What *is* a pearly queen?"

"We're the pride of London town," said Tom. "Iris, 'ere, had her costume passed down from her mother and her mother before 'er. She's true royalty is our Iris."

There was a rap at the door.

"I'll get it, luv. That'll be our Bill." Tom rose unsteadily to his feet and tottered towards the door. Voices could be heard floating along the passageway.

"There's no way that's Billy," whispered Olivia. "Sounds nothing like him."

"Plus, it's a woman," said Lissy.

"That too," replied Olivia.

"But *that's* a voice I recognize," said Aidan.

Tess bounded into the room, her face bright with excitement. "I found a friend and she's coming for tea."

Olivia gave her sister a look. "What did Mom tell you about talking to strangers?"

"She won't know if you don't tell her," said Tess. "Besides, she's not strange. She's really nice and Cagney, you are going to die when you hear her accent."

Tess broke off as an elderly lady walked into the room. She was dressed in a knee-length skirt and matching green jacket. Blue, twinkly eyes peeked from beneath a headscarf.

Iris rose to her feet, and Olivia could have sworn she saw an expression pass between the two women before Iris plunked back down.

"I believe I may have found your missing cousin," said the stranger, lowering herself into the armchair offered by Tom.

Tess bounced over to the lady and perched on her lap. "Guys, this is Lilibet. She's my new friend. She lives in London and rides horses. She's *really* cool."

"How did you find our missing friend, ma'am?" asked Tom, pouring another cup of tea and handing it to the newcomer.

"I believe she may have been trying to encourage the ravens to fly," answered Lilibet.

Iris almost choked on her chocolate biscuit.

"Quite," replied Lilibet. "Luckily, I managed to stop her in the nick of time."

"I wasn't *really* trying to get them to fly," said Tess, stealing a cookie and dunking it into Lilibet's tea. "I just felt sorry for them. I mean, it's not their problem if the monarchy falls."

"Absolutely," said Lilibet.

"But how did you know where we were?" asked Aidan.

"Tom's son was kind enough to show me where this precious child belonged."

Tess beamed at Lilibet and gave her a kiss on the cheek.

"She was trying to bring about the downfall of the monarchy," said Lissy. "I don't think she can be considered *all* that precious."

Suddenly, the door flew open. Billy stood in the opening pale faced, clutching his stomach. "Gordon Bennet, Grandad, I can't find her anywhere. Dad's gonna string me up, he will."

Tom crossed the room. "Mind ya language now, Billy. All's taken care of, and we got ourselves a visitor. Ma'am, I'd like you to meet my grandson, Billy."

Lilibet swung around and gave Billy a warm smile.

Billy's eyes nearly popped out of his head. He jabbed his finger towards Lilibet before staring wildly around the room. Slowly, he sank to his knees. "Bleedin' 'eck, Grandad. It's the queen."

11

Aftermath

J ames pulled up outside the train station and Billy was out the door in a flash. "Come on you lot, outcha get."

"Bye James," said Lissy. "Thanks for driving us around."

James held open the door and bowed slightly. "A pleasure, madam."

"All right, all right, that's enough. Let's get you lot on the train before you cause me any more trouble." Billy herded all five towards the cavernous building.

It was the day after what would be forever referred to as the 'chocolate biscuit incident.' On hearing she was sitting on the reigning monarch's lap, Tess had turned ashen. Her cookie had paused mid-way to her lips and, in one fluid motion, Tess had slid off Lilibet's lap and crumpled onto the carpet.

Tess had eventually been roused with four strong cups of tea, fifteen chocolate biscuits and a cheese and pickle sandwich. After being assured Tess was in no danger, the queen had finally departed. Tess had been in a state of shock ever since.

Billy had taken no more chances. Bundling the cousins into the Rolls, they had driven straight to the Featherington-Twits' London residence, where Billy had greeted all requests to see more of London with a serious coughing fit and a nervous giggle.

First thing the next morning, Billy had hustled them back into the Rolls and instructed James to take them straight to Kings Cross.

"Get a move on," said Billy, ushering them towards the station. "I'm not having you miss this train. I'm in enough trouble as it is."

"Aren't you coming with us, Billy?" asked Tess.

Billy let out a high-pitched laugh, scaring a cyclist and several pigeons. "Bleedin' 'eck, no."

"So, we're going on the train by ourselves?" asked Cagney.

"You got that right, missus."

The cousins trotted behind Billy, dragging their suitcases behind them. Once their tickets were purchased, Billy finally slowed his pace. "This 'ere's it. Platform ten, the 9:15 to York. Now I'm free to live a normal life without you lot destroying both me *and* the monarchy."

Lissy surveyed Billy's tense face. "Are we really *that* bad?"

"Bad! Bad?" Billy's voice rose. "She gets 'er head stuck in the bars at Buck House." Billy pointed accusingly at Tess. "And she ..." Billy continued to point at Tess, "tries to get the bloomin' ravens to fly the coop." Billy flailed his arm around wildly searching for another cousin to point at, but in the end he returned to Tess. "And *then* she manages to befriend the woman she's trying to defrone before dropping a soggy chocolate biscuit onto the queen's lap."

"So, basically it's just Tess," said Cagney. "I knew as much."

"Get on the train, will ya?" He passed Cagney a piece of paper. "Get off 'ere and Callie'll be there to pick you up. And good bleedin' luck to 'er."

The cousins waved goodbye to Billy and hurried onto the platform. Cagney led everyone along the side of the train until they found an empty carriage.

The compartment consisted of several seats, each clustered in groups of four around a table. Aidan wondered if this journey would be like the one in India. He sincerely hoped not.

Within seconds the cousins were involved in their own activities. Cagney checked her pictures. Aidan opened a book from Billy entitled *Cockney Rhyming Slang* and Olivia gazed out the window watching mice run along the tracks.

Lissy flipped open Spider's monitor and examined her watch. "Two minutes and we should be out of here." She glanced at the others. "Are we *really* as bad as Billy said?"

"*We're* not. Just the loud pink one," said Olivia.

"But Tess doesn't mean to get in trouble, do you, Tess? She just can't seem to help her ..." Lissy surveyed the carriage. She peeked under the table. "Guys?"

Lissy stared at her watch. It was one minute until 9:15 and Tess was nowhere in sight.

12

Northwood Bound

All four cousins hurried to the end of the corridor. One by one their heads darted out the window. Lissy forced down the door handle, and toppled onto the platform. The whistle blew and the train sprang forward with an almighty lurch.

Aidan reached out his hand. "Quick, get back on."

Lissy shook her head. "We can't leave her."

Olivia shrugged. "They'll be another train in a couple of days. She can get that one."

Lissy glared. "You *can't* be serious."

The train started to gather speed. Lissy broke into a trot.

"Lissy, really. You've got to get back on," said Aidan. "We'll get off at the next stop and come back. But we can't split up. It's bad enough losing Tess; we can't lose you as well."

"I'm telling you, she'll turn up," yelled Olivia. "Trust me on this."

Lissy was not convinced.

"Think of Spider," said Aidan.

Lissy's eyes bulged. She glanced through the window and saw her beloved laptop abandoned on the table. Lissy pounded down the platform towards the door. Her fingers clutched Aidan's, and he yanked her inside.

Lissy slumped into a heap, head in hands. "I can't believe we've lost her."

"Lost who?"

Lissy looked up. Standing in the corridor, her mouth full of apple, her pink skirt billowing in the breeze, stood Tess. Lissy didn't know whether to hug her or hit her.

Lissy scrambled to her feet "Where *were* you?"

"I tried to find Platform Nine and Three-Quarters."

"What?" said Lissy, straightening her headband.

"I told you we couldn't lose her." Olivia rolled her eyes. "Goodness knows I've tried."

Tess flounced along the aisle and plopped herself into a bristly blue seat.

Aidan perched on the table. "Tess, you know Platform Nine and Three-Quarters is make believe, right?"

Tess shoved the rest of the apple into her mouth, core and all, and gave it a good crunch. "I know, but there's no harm in making sure."

Lissy shook her head. "You nearly gave me a heart attack."

"That's what the porter said when he saw me running at the wall with a trolley."

"Was he mad?" asked Olivia, hopefully.

"Nope! Actually, he said people do it all the time. But not often with so much enthusiasm."

Cagney turned to Olivia. "She's crazy, you know. Quite crazy."

Tess grinned at Cagney. "Lilibet didn't think I was crazy. Lilibet said I was—"

Cagney rolled her eyes. "Believe me, we remember. She said you were ..." Cagney almost choked on the word, "precious."

"Yep. After having all those crowns and stuff going missing, Lilibet said I was just the tonic she needed."

"She was in shock," said Olivia. "I mean, imagine waking up one morning with half your headgear missing - it must have affected her brain."

Lissy stared at Tess. "How do you know the crowns went missing, Tess? Kevin wouldn't tell us what had been stolen, and it's never been fully explained in the papers. They've all been so vague."

"Lilibet told me on the way to Tom and Iris'. She said someone had stolen three crowns, plus the scepter and an orb." Tess stuffed half a banana into her mouth. "By the way, what's an orb? Come to think of it, what's a scepter?"

Lissy swung Spider around to face Tess. The screen featured a picture of a much younger Lilibet sitting on a throne. A sparkling crown dwarfed her dark curls, a long cape cascaded over her shoulders. In her left hand was an ornate gold ball, much larger than an orange. In her right she held a long stick that, if dropped, could seriously damage someone's head.

"That's Lilibet?" Tess leaned forward to get a better view. "Wow! She looks good without a headscarf."

"This was her coronation day, back in 1953. She was only twenty-seven when she was crowned queen. She's wearing St. Edward's crown, and see what she's holding in her hands?" said Lissy. "That's the orb and scepter."

"They're pretty," said Tess. "I bet they cost a lot."

Lissy smiled. "I'm pretty sure they're priceless. The crown is made of solid gold and has four-hundred-and-forty precious stones. The border is made of ermine, a kind of fur, and the whole crown weighs almost five pounds."

"That's like having a bag of potatoes on your head," said Olivia.

"Wow," said Tess. "Lilibet must be strong."

"It says she practiced wearing it for weeks before the coronation to get used to the weight," said Lissy.

Tess smiled as she envisioned Lilibet wandering around the palace in pajamas, a crown stuffed on her head.

The previous day was still vivid in Lissy's mind. When Tess first hit the floor Lissy, along with the others, assumed she was faking. However, explaining Tess' tendency to pretend to faint seemed more than a little complicated.

Unfortunately, at that point the queen had dropped to her knees and started listening for a heartbeat. It was a moment Lissy would remember with horror for the rest of her life. *What must the queen have thought of them?* Lissy didn't want to think about it.

When Tess finally opened her eyes, Lilibet had scooped her into her arms and given her a giant bear hug. It was official. Tess, in her affable, kind-hearted way, had won the affection of the Queen of England. After promises of tea and scones at the palace, the queen had departed.

"I still say the woman was in shock," said Cagney. "I mean no one in their right mind is going to invite *that* to the palace." Cagney's gaze landed on Tess, who was busy massacring a jelly donut.

Lissy sniffed. "You're just jealous because you met the queen in puddle jeans."

Cagney blushed at the memory. If Cagney had ever envisioned meeting royalty it had never been while wearing jeans that had recently done battle with a puddle and hair in desperate need of a hat. Cagney, like Lissy, was trying her best to put yesterday out of her mind.

The London skyline gave way to a softer landscape and the cousins settled into their pursuits. Pretty soon it was more common to see a field of sheep than a city of skyscrapers. The scenery wasn't dramatic, but it was pleasant and green. The gentle rocking motion of the train soon lulled everyone into silence and soon after that - sleep.

It was the lurch of the train that woke Cagney. Slowly, she opened her eyes. The train was pulling out of a station. Adjusting her glasses, she peered out the window and read the sign. There was something very familiar about it. Something she'd seen before. Cagney reached into her pocket and pulled out the piece of paper Billy had given her. A second later she stood so fast she smacked her knees into the table. "Move!" she screamed.

Aidan's eyes shot open. "Who is it? Where is it?" Aidan stared out the window and saw the passing sign. "Guys! Quick!" Aidan shook Olivia and Tess, while Lissy was lulled back to consciousness by Cagney climbing over her head.

Half kicking, half dragging, Aidan maneuvered the bags through the carriage. He reached the door of the train, slung it open and flung the bags onto the platform. "Jump!" he yelled.

Olivia went first, followed by Tess. Cagney paused in the doorway, but a quick kick to her rear had her flying out the door. Lissy finally appeared clutching Spider beneath her arm. Aidan grasped her hand and together they jumped.

The cousins lay scattered along the platform like confetti.

Cagney rolled herself out of a large, muddy puddle and scrambled to her knees. Yet another pair of jeans ruined, and her jacket wasn't faring too well either. At least there were no witnesses this time.

They'd been so late getting off the train the entire platform lay empty.

Cagney flipped herself around and saw a dozen pairs of eyes watching. *Her* side of the platform may have been empty, but the other side wasn't. In fact, there were several people who were out and out staring. A teenage girl giggled. A man in a business suit held up a cell phone and snapped pictures. Behind them, Cagney could just make out an older lady who was glaring across the train tracks.

Cagney was suddenly aware of a clinking sound as the southbound train rumbled into the station. Cagney pulled herself to her feet. She removed a leaf, a twig and something sticky from her curls. Thirty seconds later the train pulled out. Cagney scanned the platform, but the platform had emptied. Grandma was gone.

13

Featherington-Twit

The cousins gathered their bags and headed towards the exit. It was a sweet little station, old-fashioned and quaint. The cousins reached the lobby, but found no one to take their tickets. In fact, the station seemed quite deserted. Cagney deposited their tickets in the trash and strolled through the exit.

A small parking lot stretched ahead. Olivia recognized the famous English mini and some Volkswagen bugs, plus cars, so tiny, she wondered if they were for children. There wasn't a truck, SUV or minivan in sight. In fact, there wasn't *anyone* in sight, not a shop, not a pigeon, not a soul. Beyond the parking lot lay a small country road and fields surrounded by a tall hedge. Olivia thought she could hear the sound of mooing. She sniffed the air. Yep, definitely mooing.

Lissy slumped onto a bench. "I don't know why I'm surprised. I mean, did any of us really expect Grandma to be here?"

"I did," said Tess. "I was all ready to tell her about my—"

Olivia tugged one of Tess' pigtails. "She's probably just late."

"I don't think so," said Cagney, flicking dirt off her jeans. "In fact, I think I just saw her heading south on the London train."

"What?" Lissy leapt to her feet. "How are we ever going to figure out what's going on. I swear, grown-ups are the most selfish, inconsiderate, low-down ..."

Aidan laid a hand on Lissy's shoulder. "Down, tiger."

Lissy slumped back onto the bench. "Fine! I'm calm, but *now* what do we do? Here we are in the middle of—" Lissy blew a stray curl off her face. "Where are we?"

Cagney took a deep breath and tried to muster some dignity. "Bumble Bottom."

Lissy gazed at her incredulously. "Don't mess with me, Cagney Puddleton. Where are we?"

Cagney scowled. "I'm just telling you what the sign says."

Lissy swiveled to see a white sign with black peeling paint. Written on it, as clear as mud, were the words *Bumble Bottom.*

Olivia trawled her fingers through her unbrushed hair. "Is it some kind of joke they play on tourists? I mean, who names a town 'Bumble Bottom'? It's like something out of Winnie the Pooh."

Aidan lowered the schedule he'd been reading. "Well, wherever we are, we're stuck. The next train to London doesn't come through 'til tomorrow."

Lissy sucked in air. "I swear I'm going to—"

Aidan cut her off. "Maybe if we start walking we'll get to a village or something? Come on. It's not so bad. We've been stranded in far worse places."

Lissy allowed herself to be pulled to her feet. Cagney wished for the thousandth time she'd packed lighter, although, at the rate she was destroying jeans, she would need every last pair. The thought of trudging along a country lane searching for some kind of bumbling village did not fill her with joy, but at least it wasn't raining. Cagney inspected the cloudy sky - at least it wasn't raining - yet.

"We could ask *him* where the village is," said Tess.

Cagney rolled her eyes. "Ask who?"

"Him." Tess pointed to a car at the far end of the parking lot.

Cagney adjusted her glasses and squinted towards the only car bigger than a fridge. Tess was right. There was definitely someone in it. Cagney grabbed her bags and took off across the forecourt.

It was an unusual car, with a tire sitting on the hood and a roof made of canvas. The vehicle gave the impression of once being green, but it was so splattered in mud, it was hard to tell. Cagney peered in the open window. She peered closer. An elderly man lay slumped behind the wheel, a forgotten newspaper across his chest.

Olivia leaned forward and whispered in Cagney's ear. "He's not dead is he?"

Cagney leapt back, lost her footing and headed bottom-first towards another murky puddle.

Aidan grabbed his sister and hauled her to a standing position. "You're welcome," he muttered, as his sister disentangled herself from his grip.

Tess pointed towards the rise and fall of the newspaper. "He's not dead. He's sleeping."

The cousins crowded around the vehicle.

"Should we wake him?" whispered Lissy.

"Sure." Tess reached in and leaned on the steering wheel. The sound of a horn blasted through the parking lot. The man still didn't move.

"Wow!" said Tess. "Maybe he *is* dead."

"Not dead," came a reply. "But luckily slightly deaf, else your wish may have come true."

Tess smiled at the twinkling blue eyes gazing upon her.

"Don't tell me, my dear - *you* must be Tess." The man settled himself upright in the seat, smoothed his newspaper and laid it beside him. Using his hands to shoo the cousins back, he opened the door and unfolded himself from within.

A pair of mud-encrusted boots emerged first, followed by incredibly long legs. The man stood at least six-and-a-half feet tall and towered over the cousins. He wore an outfit that, although scruffy, screamed country gentleman. Cagney did not know what tweed was, but she'd bet her entire *Clamour* collection this man was wearing it.

The man raised his hat. "Featherington-Twit, at your service."

The man's voice resonated deep and strong. It had command to it, and Aidan wondered if the elderly gentleman had ever been in the Army. Despite the muddy boots and strange suit, Aidan decided he looked very regimental.

Cagney knew her cue. She quickly introduced each cousin, to whom the old man raised his hat in turn.

"Just saw Callie onto the 5:15 to London. Amazing woman." He cleared his throat. "Must have dozed off for a bit. Oh well, no harm done, you're here now. Going to be staying with us for a while, if that's okay?" He stuck out his arm and studied his watch. "Better get a move on. Henri's dying to meet you and Carrington does get dreadfully put out if we're late for dinner."

Featherington-Twit opened the door and wedged himself behind the driver's seat. "Jump in and we'll be off."

Lissy gaped at the others, who were slinging their bags through the back door of the Jeep. Were they really going to get into this mud-encrusted scrap of junk with a complete stranger? Aidan gave her a reassuring smile. She sighed. To be honest, they'd done worse.

Reluctantly, Lissy clambered into the back of what had to be the oldest Jeep in the history of the universe. Basic didn't begin to describe it. The two seats, running down either side of the vehicle, consisted of little more than a bench, plus there was an overwhelming smell of damp dog. By the length of the dog hair, a *large* damp dog.

"Everyone in? Good. Off to the shack, it is, then."

Featherington-Twit grinded the stick-shift into reverse. Signaling, he swerved into the narrow lane and hung a left.

Cagney leaned forward. "Is it far to the ... erm, shack?"

Featherington-Twit shook his head. "Just through the village."

Cagney slunk back onto the bench. Great. Not only had they been shipped off to the country, they were now expected to stay in a shack. Cagney wished, not for the first time this summer, to be back in Texas - even if it was hotter than a billy goat in a pepper patch.

Featherington-Twit steered the Jeep down the winding road. Aidan tried to see out, but the dirt-smeared windows made it almost impossible. They seemed to be surrounded by a green hedge looming high on each side. The lane itself was so narrow Aidan dreaded to think what would happen if they met another vehicle. "Mr. Twit?"

Featherington-Twit swiveled in his seat, his blue eyes alive with curiosity. "Yes, my boy?"

"Are all the roads around here so narrow? I mean, what do you do if you meet another car?"

Featherington-Twit smiled. "You crash!"

Aidan looked horrified.

"You pull in, my son." He motioned to a small cut out Aidan hadn't seen in the hedge. "Roads dotted with them. And, if you meet someone head-to-head, so to speak, then the smaller car backs up."

"Oh!" Aidan sincerely hoped they didn't meet anything bigger than them.

"These roads have been here for hundreds of years. Potts swears he sees armies marching along this one."

"Who's Potts?" asked Tess.

"Local village idiot. Any village worth its salt has one."

"What army?" asked Olivia.

"Cromwell's," replied Featherington-Twit.

Lissy almost dropped Spider. "You mean, Oliver Cromwell?"

"Is he famous?" asked Tess.

"Back in the seventeenth century he was," replied Lissy.

"Yes! Dear old Potty is convinced he sees the army of Oliver Cromwell marching through these very lanes."

"But aren't they dead?" asked Olivia.

Featherington-Twit nodded. "As dodos."

The cousins fell silent. A few minutes later they rounded a bend and the hedge ended. A field full of cows quickly gave way to a farm, then a couple of cottages and, finally, the cousins got their first glimpse of Bumble Bottom.

The Jeep sauntered along a winding street opening onto a village green where a cricket match was taking place. The village was as tiny as its name suggested. A pub, an antique store and a church dotted the high street.

Picturesque cottages clustered around a duck pond, and a girl on a pony ambled out of a nearby lane.

Featherington-Twit changed into a lower gear and soon the idyllic village lay behind.

Cagney tapped Featherington-Twit on the shoulder. "I thought you said we were going to Bumble Bottom."

"Oh we are, my dear, we are. The shack is just up the hill. Won't be long now."

Lissy prepared herself. Featherington-Twit seemed like a nice old man. She didn't want to make him feel bad if his home was a little downtrodden. What a shame he couldn't live in one of those cute cottages with roses growing up the side. The Jeep slowed and bumped its way over a metal grate and through a pair of ornate iron gates.

On the right sat the sweetest cottage Lissy had ever seen. She wondered how they were all going to fit, but that was another matter. "Oh, it's darling," she exclaimed.

Featherington-Twit angled himself to face Lissy. "Say again?"

"Your house, it's lovely."

"What? The gatehouse? My dear child, I'm afraid that is *not* my home."

Lissy sank back onto the bench. She should have guessed. It was too good to be true.

Featherington-Twit continued down a long, straight lane. Hugging either side were oak trees at least a couple of hundred years old. Gnarly and huge, they blocked out the weak sunshine trying to push its way through the clouds.

Suddenly the texture under the wheels changed and Lissy realized they were now on gravel. She peeked out the dirt-encrusted window and this time, she did drop Spider.

*
* *

14

The Shack

L ooming in front of the Jeep rose a castle with
four turrets. A flag with a crest of arms flew
from the roof. A moat with a drawbridge
completed the fairytale abode. The Jeep scrunched
to a halt and the cousins scrambled out.

Featherington-Twit eased out of his seat and
strolled around to join them. Idly he twisted a
button dangling from his jacket.

Cagney lifted her camera and snapped. "*This* is
the shack?"

"Most certainly. Bit run down. However, we do
the best we can."

Lissy's eyes bulged. "Run down? This isn't run
down, this is ... it's ..."

"Magical," said Tess.

A cool breeze rustled through the trees as Olivia grabbed her bag and slung it across her shoulder. Instantly she felt it lift from her arms.

"If madam would be so kind."

Olivia turned. Two servants had appeared from nowhere. A maid with startling red hair wearing an old-fashioned black dress stood smiling by the car. An older man dressed in an immaculate gray suit organized the luggage. From the way he spoke he could have been James' younger brother; in fact, Olivia wasn't so sure he wasn't.

"Hey, thanks," said Olivia.

"Aaah, Carrington. I trust we are not too late for dinner."

"Right on time, ma' lord."

Cagney spun to face Featherington-Twit. "Did he say lord?"

"Carrington has a thing about titles. Wouldn't put too much stock in it, personally."

"Let me get this right." Cagney eyed the elderly man. "*You're* a lord."

"Yes. Although I believe we have already established that fact." Featherington-Twit winked at Tess.

Cagney sighed. She would never understand this British aristocracy thing. First a queen who turned up in a headscarf, now a lord who ran around in a battered Jeep wearing rain boots, or what was that word the English used? Ah, that was right, wellies. These English sure were a funny lot.

Cagney turned as another set of feet crunched across the gravel. A stout woman with pale white hair pulled into a loose bun bustled towards them. She wore a practical, no-nonsense suit and her voice, when it came, was decisive and loud.

"I say, don't bore them, Basil. Carrington, take the bags to the south wing, if you'd be so kind."

Cagney's eyebrows rose to epic heights. There was a south wing? She raised her camera and fired off several shots. Now *this* was more like it.

"Yes, ma' lady," said Carrington.

"And for goodness sake, Basil, go change. You'll lose that button and then there'll be heck to pay."

"Yes, dear." The lord of the manor retrieved his newspaper before crunching across the gravel towards the drawbridge.

Tess' eyes bulged even wider. "Ma lady?"

"Oh don't mind Carrington. He's a frightful snob. Call me Henri. Short for Henrietta. Dreadful name, isn't it? Sounds like a boat race."

Olivia smiled. She had a feeling she was going to like Henri.

"How was the journey? Dreadful, I know. Lucky to get you here at all. All those train strikes." Lady Henrietta Featherington-Twit linked arms with Tess and strolled towards the moat.

"Is this a real castle?" asked Tess. "You know, like Cinderella's?"

Henri let out a guffaw of laughter. "Guess you could say that. Been in Basil's family for donkey's years. Bit of a liability really. I'd be quite happy in a small cottage with a holiday villa in Spain, but Basil won't hear of it. He complains, of course. Roof leaks, central heating hangs on by a lick and a prayer, but he loves the old place really."

Henri ushered Tess over the drawbridge and into a cobbled courtyard. Tess was so happy her knees felt weak and her hand felt wet. Tess looked down to see a dopey looking bloodhound licking her fingers.

"Oooh, hello." Tess dropped to her knees and gave the dog a pat. Tess was rewarded with a slobbering lick from chin to cheek.

"Basil!" yelled Henri. "Control your blasted animal."

"I don't mind. I love dogs," said Tess, trying to fend off several enthusiastic kisses.

"Baskerville, sit!" commanded Henri. Baskerville toppled Tess to the cobblestones, sniffing her pink raincoat with enthusiasm.

"He must smell something. Filthy scavenger. You don't happen to have any food on you, do you?"

Cagney rolled her eyes. "Little do you know."

Tess routed around in her pocket and pulled out half a jelly donut. Baskerville plucked it from her fingers, downing it in one gulp before bounding back across the drawbridge.

Aidan helped Tess to her feet.

Tess grinned. "I like him."

"Nasty, rotten brute, but Basil's rather fond of him."

Olivia could see why. Baskerville was large and enthusiastic - just what a dog should be.

"I say, fancy a quick tour?" Henri strode across the courtyard and disappeared through a studded wooden door.

The cousins tore after her, jostling for position until all five filled the doorway. With a heave, they burst into the entryway.

Lissy gasped. She felt like she'd tumbled through time.

Henri stood halfway along a paneled corridor. "Come on, chaps, don't dawdle."

The cousins hurried along the hallway. A narrow wooden table stretched from one end of the passageway to the other. On the opposite wall hung a large embroidered blanket. Lissy traced a finger over the heavy fabric.

"Tapestries," explained Henri. "Back in the fifteen-hundreds they were the equivalent of indoor heating."

Passing through the hallway, the five followed Henri into an ornate living room. Lissy could tell it was a living room from the high-backed sofa positioned in front of a fireplace *so* large it could do double duty as a soccer goal. Leaded glass windows dotted the stone walls, two enormous suits of armor loomed in the corners and life-sized paintings of men in stiff collars hung from high ceilings.

"Basil's lot." Henri indicated the portraits. "Motley crew, aren't they?"

Olivia paused to examine the drawing of a pious looking bishop.

"Don't let the dog collar fool you, dear." Henri crossed the room. "*He* was the worst of the bunch."

Lissy gazed around the room. Only one table held any reminder of modern day life. Lissy grasped one of several black-and-white framed photographs.

The features of Lord and Lady Featherington-Twit smiled up at her from the frame. It had obviously been taken many years ago as not only were the Featherington-Twits much younger, but an impish looking boy in shorts sprawled happily across Henri's lap.

Lissy felt the picture rise from her fingers and Henri replaced it on the table.

"Is that your son?" asked Lissy.

"Yes, that's William. Wonderful boy."

"Does he live close by?" asked Lissy.

"Died, many years ago now. Still hurts. A mother's love, and all that. But he was a fine man and we got to see him marry and be happy, and for that I'm thankful." Henri turned to face the others who were gazing at the portraits filling the walls.

"Who's this?" Tess stood in front of a large gold-framed painting. It featured a woman standing at a window, her hair so blonde it was almost white. Her face was ashen and, to complete the illusion of ghostliness, she wore a shapeless white dress. "Is she going to bed?"

"Fashion of the day." Henri smoothed down her own green suit. "Rather impractical if you ask me."

"Why's she so sad?" asked Lissy.

"Legend has it, the man she loved was promised to someone else."

"Oh, that *is* sad," said Tess.

"Anyhow, silly cow never got over it. Jumped off the battlement not a year after this was painted."

"Was she hurt?" asked Tess.

"You could say that." Henri cleared her throat. "In fact, her ghost is supposed to haunt the south wing."

Cagney snorted. She didn't believe in ghosts and scorned those who did.

"You mean the south wing where we're sleeping?" asked Lissy, with a gulp.

"Yes, yes. All a bunch of codswallop, if you ask me. Lived here more than half my life, never seen so much as a glimpse of her. Superstitious nonsense. Although the servants all swear they've seen her." Henri flung open a door, letting in a cool summer breeze. "Personally, I think they're imagining things."

Lissy felt goose bumps rise on her arms. All this talk of ghosts made her uneasy. Lissy turned. A servant with red hair and startling green eyes stood lingering by the door, obviously waiting to come into the room. Taking one last glance at the portrait of the lady in white, Lissy bounded after the others.

She caught up with them as Henri breezed through a formal dining room and onto a patio.

The patio consisted of a long stone balcony set several feet off the ground with wide, shallow steps fanning out to the lawn below. The grass gave way to a field with several black and white cows. Beyond the field lay a forest. It was all so very picturesque.

Plopped in the middle of the patio sat a neat little table holding a crystal jug and matching glasses. Henri deposited herself at the top of the table and the cousins pulled out chairs and sat beside her.

"Oooh! Pink lemonade." Tess reached for a glass, but Lissy beat her to it. Tess and crystal was never a good combination. Standing, Lissy poured Tess and everyone else a tumbler full of pink liquid.

Henri reached under the table and brought out a horn with a black squeezy end. She handed it to Olivia. "Would you be a dear? Two blasts should be enough."

Olivia clasped the horn and gave it a good squeeze. The horn let out an almighty honk. Olivia did it again. She was beginning to like the English. They were crazy, for sure, but she'd lived with crazy long enough to recognize and enjoy it when it came to visit.

Seconds later, Carrington appeared at the door.

"You called, madam."

"Carrington, I think snacks might be in order."

"Right away, madam."

Lissy took a deep breath and asked the question that had been on her mind since leaving the station. "Lady Featherington-Twit, when are we going to see our grandma?"

"Aah, yes. Excellent question." Henri reached for her drink. Immediately her concentration seemed lost as she stared over Lissy's head. "Darn and blast the man."

Lissy swiveled and followed Henri's gaze.

Striding across the lawn came a ruddy-faced man with three stout dogs trotting at his feet. He wore a blue blazer and a bright yellow scarf around his neck. Aiding his progress was a cane, which he thrust forward and into the ground at regular intervals.

"It's just too bad." Henri sniffed. "Can't be helped, I suppose. Can only hope Basil is still changing. Can't stand the man. Don't blame him. Dreadful bore."

"Who's a dreadful bore?" asked Tess, eyeing the remainder of the lemonade.

Henri looked confused. "Right. Course. Never met him, have you? Major Percival Puffin. Bore you to tears just to look at him."

"But why's he walking across your backyard?" Aidan observed the man hastening towards them. "Isn't it private?"

"Should be, shouldn't it? A woman's castle is her home and all that." Henri chuckled. "Public right of way, though. Runs through the entire forest. Been there for centuries. Can't do a darn thing about it."

"But he's not walking in the forest," said Lissy. "He's coming right towards us."

Henri slugged back the rest of her drink. "News of your arrival probably spread. Not much gets by in a village this small. Biggest gossip in three counties is Puffin."

Major Puffin grew closer. He waved his stick in greeting but suddenly stopped. His stick ceased waggling and slowly he raised his other hand. His dogs started to whimper and the largest of the three turned tail and lollopped towards the forest.

"I say, what's the stupid man doing?" Henri rose to her feet.

Aidan frowned. "I think he's surrendering."

"Surrendering to whom?" Henri's voice rose. "Silly man. You're not in the Army now you know, Puffin."

Tess pointed towards the castle. "I could be wrong, but I think he's surrendering to the guy with the gun."

15

Terror

Tess dove under the table. With her pink fluffy skirt sticking skyward, she resembled an exotic bird burrowing for food. Aidan launched himself towards his sister. Cagney crumpled with a muffled cry as her brother hit her smack in the stomach. Lissy dropped into a turtle position and placed her hands over her head. Only Olivia and Henri remained standing.

There was an eerie silence, shattered first by a howl and then by the sound of the overturned pitcher splattering droplets. When the gun went off, it blasted so loud Aidan feared for his hearing. He glanced up to see a man's feet heading towards him. Helpless, Aidan wished he'd been a better brother. He was about to express this sentiment when the gun went off again. There was silence. Then Aidan heard screaming.

Tess peeked around the table legs. She stuck a finger in her ear and gave it a good wiggle. From her position - nose down on the patio - she couldn't see much. Feet. She could see lots of feet, plus Cagney batting Aidan around the head as she tried to heave him off of her tummy. Tess felt a shiver run down her spine. Scrambling to her knees, she took in the scene. Olivia and the maid with bright red hair stood calmly by the top of the steps. To the right stood Henri, not quite so calm. In fact Henri seemed annoyed - very annoyed. With her mouth ajar and her arms flailing, she was obviously yelling at someone. But who?

Olivia froze, too stunned to move. Focusing on the French windows she squinted against the sunlight. Rats. This country had been shrouded in gray since touching down at Heathrow. Trust the sun to finally make an appearance when she needed to see clearly. With the sunlight glinting off the glass it was impossible to see who the gunman was. Growing up in Texas Olivia wasn't afraid of guns, but she had a healthy respect for them. Olivia rarely got scared. As the gunman bounded towards her, she started to rethink this policy.

Lissy unfurled from her tortoise position and risked peeking through the table legs. The first thing she saw was a ball of pink fluff quivering like Jell-O. Good, that meant Tess was okay. She peered over to see Cagney on top of Aidan stabbing a finger towards his forehead. They, too, seemed to have escaped unharmed. Lissy suddenly became aware of yelling. She glanced around searching for the source. Finding it, she decided to resume being a turtle.

Slowly, someone else's words broke through Cagney's tirade. She stopped batting her brother around the head and listened.

"Blithering idiot ... of all the foolhardy, idiotic, numbskull ..." The words flew so fast they blended together.

Cagney tried to make out the source of all the shouting, but before she could make an informed decision, she heard footsteps pounding in her direction. Cagney glanced up and saw the man with the rifle striding towards her. In one motion she rolled onto her back and pulled Aidan on top. Heck, if Aidan wanted to protect her, who was she to stop him?

Henri's words continued to fly. The words 'nitwit' and 'nincompoop' were particularly appealing to Tess and she made a mental note to look up some of the words once she got back to Texas and try them out on her classmates next year.

It wasn't until the gunman came level with Olivia that she could actually see who it was. Henri stuck out a foot to trip him, but, with an agility that defied his age, Lord Featherington-Twit sideswiped Henri's shoe and plunged down the patio steps.

It was quite clear now who the lord was shooting at, but why? Surely being boring wasn't *that* much of a crime?

"I say, get down." Henri waved her arms frantically. "Get down, you blithering idiot."

Major Puffin stood motionless. He held his cane aloft, sword-like and blinked several times. It appeared to Olivia that he was resigned to his fate. In fact, if it hadn't been for the one remaining dog quivering between his legs, he might have looked quite gallant.

Henri dashed after her husband. "Are you deaf, man? Ground Puffin. Hit the ground!"

It was obvious Lord Featherington-Twit had completely lost it. Olivia shook her head. You just couldn't tell who the crazy ones were. Olivia spied a mound of pink tulle underneath the table. Of course, there *were* exceptions.

Olivia watched Featherington-Twit charge across the lawn, the distance between the two men narrowing by the second. The others scrambled to their feet and joined her to watch from the patio. Major Puffin stood on the lawn, indignation blanketing his face. If it wasn't so terrifying it might have been comical.

His rifle slung over his shoulder, Lord Featherington-Twit was gaining ground. Finally there was Henri, chasing behind him, yelling words the cousins had been told never to use.

"Oooh!" Tess shook her head. "It doesn't look good for the guy with the stick, right Olivia?"

Aidan rubbed the point on his forehead where Cagney had poked it. "I wouldn't put my money on him."

A second howl pierced the air. The cousins spun to face the castle. Baskerville stood on the patio, his head thrown back, his ears flapping in the breeze. He let out another mournful wail before scampering down the steps after his master.

Olivia grinned. "This just gets better."

"Olivia!" Lissy was shocked. "That poor man, he's helpless."

"He could run," suggested Cagney.

"I think he's in shock," said Aidan.

"You'd be in shock if someone took pot shots at you," said Olivia.

Any second now Featherington-Twit would reach his target. Lissy buried her face into Aidan's shoulder. "I can't look. Tell me when he's dead."

"Not dead yet," said Tess. "Or yet. Or ..."

Cagney punched Tess in the arm.

Aidan wondered why Featherington-Twit had not taken aim before. Surely he couldn't miss at such short distance. But still he continued doggedly towards the quivering man. Closer and closer until Aidan thought they were going to collide. And then, the most extraordinary thing happened. Featherington-Twit kept on running.

"Mr. Twit, you missed him," yelled Tess.

Cagney clapped a hand over Tess' mouth. "Be quiet, do you *want* him to get shot?"

"Oooh!" mumbled Tess. "I hadn't thought of that."

Olivia frowned. "Where's he going?"

Lissy unburied her head. "Looks like he's heading for the trees."

No sooner had Lissy spoken than once again Featherington-Twit paused, took aim and fired.

Aidan scratched his head. "Who's he shooting at?"

Olivia surveyed the forest. A flash of red disappeared behind a clump of trees. "I think there's someone in the woods."

Lissy saw the red too. "Maybe a poacher?"

"Do you think he's going to be all right?" asked Tess.

"He's got a rifle," said Cagney. "Of *course* he's going to be all right."

"Not Lord Featherington-Twit. Him." Tess pointed to where Henri knelt over the limp body of Major Percival Puffin.

16

Percival Puffin

The cousins tore down the steps and flew across the lawn to where Henri hovered over the body of Major Puffin.

Lissy shut her eyes. "Is he dead?"

Henri seemed surprised. "Course not. Just fainted. Wake up, man. You're perfectly all right. 'Though he's lucky Basil didn't shoot him. Man's a dreadful shot. Poor darling couldn't hit his own foot."

Olivia frowned. "Then who was he firing at?"

"Darned fox, of course. Drives Baskerville completely insane."

"Oh!" the cousins said as one.

Henri chuckled. "You didn't think Basil was shooting at Puffin here, did you?"

Lissy's cheeks flushed.

"Basil wouldn't hurt a fly."

"He was shooting at a fox," said Tess.

"Hmm! Well pointed out." Henri grabbed Major Puffin and gave him a good shake. "Although I don't think he was actually trying to kill it. Just scare it," Henri added.

"Scared me," said Lissy.

Henri surveyed the Major. "Mind you, probably a good idea to fire a few warning shots. Might stop people traipsing across our lawn whenever the fancy takes them. Hey, Puffin?"

"I was not traipsing, madam. A member of Her Majesty's Royal Artillery does not traipse."

"Ah, you're back with us. Foolhardy thing to do, getting between Basil and his wretched fox. Lucky Basil didn't shoot *you*. Course, if you'd listened to me and hit the ground, whole incident could have been avoided."

"Neither do members of Her Majesty's Royal Artillery 'hit the ground'."

Cagney eyed the major, lying flat on his back. "You're on the ground now, aren't you?"

Major Puffin struggled to his elbows. "Who, the blazes, are you?"

Cagney was about to tell him when Major Puffin waggled his hand in Cagney's direction. "Don't just stand there, woman. Help me up."

Cagney reached down, grasped the major's walking stick, and pulled. The major lifted roughly one inch off the ground.

"Put your back into it, woman!" barked the major.

Cagney growled. Olivia hid a smile.

"Aidan, why don't you help her?" said Lissy, who would have helped herself but was scared of the gruff man with the cane.

Aidan rubbed the point on his forehead where Cagney had poked him. "Aah, she's doing fine, aren't you, sis?"

Cagney growled louder.

Tess bounded towards the major. "I'll help."

Major Puffin's eyes bulged as he viewed the vision in pink bounding towards him. "What, the devil, is that?"

"*That* is what you'd call a Tess," said Aidan.

"Come, Mr. Puffin, take my hand." Tess reached down and placed her small hand into his.

Somewhat taken aback, Major Puffin clasped Tess' hand and struggled to his feet. He brushed down his blazer and regained a look of indignation.

A muffled howl rose from the woods. Major Puffin and his cane swung to face the forest, missing Cagney by inches.

Cagney glared at the major, as yet another shot echoed through the evening air.

Puffin circled his walking stick over his head. "Is the man crazy?"

"He's been saner," replied Henri.

As if they'd been let loose from a starting gate, two small dogs emerged from the forest and hurtled across the lawn. Major Puffin sank to his knees and opened his arms. "Windsor, my boy. Balmoral, come to daddy."

Olivia stifled a laugh. Olivia was an animal lover but she would never tell Rufus to 'come to mummy'. That was for sissy dogs.

The sandy colored dogs streaked towards the major as fast as their stubby legs would allow.

"I thought Windsor and Balmoral were royal castles," said Lissy.

"Certainly are, young lady." The major indicated the third dog. "This young chap here is Buckingham."

Henri rolled her eyes. "Puffin, here, is a regular royal lover, aren't you, Puffin?"

"And proud of it, madam. Proud of it."

Twenty minutes later, Henri, the cousins, Major Puffin and his three corgis were situated on the patio. Carrington had replaced the pitcher, and calm had been restored.

Major Puffin took a sip of his drink and returned to the conversation he'd been dominating since regaining a vertical position. Olivia had never heard anyone talk so much about so little. She surveyed the others. Tess' head lay on the table. Aidan's expression was glazed. Cagney's arms wove tight across her chest and Lissy slumped in her seat, her eyes firmly shut. Henri downed her drink and peered anxiously into the forest.

"Where was I, where was I?" droned the major.

Aidan started to wish Featherington-Twit *had* shot him. Nowhere deadly of course, but maybe then the man would stop talking.

Major Puffin bent down and ruffled Balmoral's ear. "Oh yes, as I was saying. Struck the blighter in the hoozame whatzits. Was the last time we saw him, *or* his band of rapscallions."

Cagney groaned. The major flashed Cagney a disapproving stare. "Of course, that was before I became one of the queen's bodyguards."

Tess lifted her head. "You were a bodyguard to the queen? A guard at the Tower, like Kevin?"

Aidan's eyes came back into focus.

Major P. plumped out his chest. "Quite so, quite so. And proud to do it, mind. Proud to do it."

"So what do you think about the crown jewels being stolen?" asked Aidan.

The major raised his cane and shook it. Cagney ducked. "Traitors! If I ever get my hands on the fiends, I'll ... I'll ..."

Henri up-ended the pitcher and shook the last few drops into her glass. "Yes, yes, Puffin, we know."

"Dirty, rotten, no good ..."

"How do you think they did it?" asked Olivia. "I mean, their security must be the best, right?"

"Of course, young man. Oversaw the whole kit and caboodle myself. No way the jewel house could ever be compromised."

Aidan smiled. Olivia's gender was constantly confused. With her short, dark hair and clothes more common to boys than girls, it was an easy mistake.

"Would you consider having the crown jewels stolen compromised or *not* compromised?" asked Tess.

Pink liquid sprayed like a garden hose from the major's nose. "Darn and blast the child." The major reached for a napkin and blotted his shirt. "Inside job! Must have been."

"You're saying you think a *guard* stole the crown jewels?" asked Olivia.

The major had been red before, now he looked close to exploding. "What did he say?"

Lissy shot Olivia a warning look. "I think my cousin was trying to say that if the security is unbreakable, how did the crown jewels get stolen?"

Major Puffin shook his head. "Darn mystery to me."

"Did the police come and interview you?" asked Aidan.

"Got myself on the first train to London. Minute I heard about it. Went straight to Scotland Yard. Told them everything I know."

"That must have taken a while," whispered Cagney.

"What she say?" asked the major, cupping his ear.

"She said, that was nice of you," answered Lissy.

"Least I could do. Nobody knows the Tower's security system like I do. Was there from start to finish. Soup to nuts, you might say. In fact, there are things that *only* I know."

"Oooh!" said Tess. "Like what?"

Major Puffin looked rather smug. "Well, you know. Things." He tapped the side of his nose. "Tricks of the trade you might say. It's not all high-tech security you know. There was this one time—"

Henri stood so quickly her chair toppled backwards. "I say, Basil! Woo hoo!"

"Oh no," Lissy clapped a hand over her eyes. "Tell me he doesn't have a dead fox. I couldn't bear it."

Olivia surveyed the forest where she could just see a flash of red disappear into the clearing. She smiled. It seemed the rascally fox would live another day.

17

The Boxing Match

Lord Featherington-Twit trudged across the lawn looking as dejected as his dog. "Blasted creature, Henri. Upsetting Baskerville."

"There, there dear, couldn't be helped. Did your best."

Featherington-Twit reached the top step and rested his gun against the balustrade.

"Don't you worry yourself. You'll scare him away sooner or later. Here, have yourself a drink." Henri lifted the pitcher and realized it was empty. Reaching under the table, Henri blasted off two more honks on the horn.

"Glad to see you back, Basil. Puffin here's been telling our American friends *all* about his time at the Tower."

Featherington-Twit rolled his eyes. "Never miss an opportunity to tell a story, ay, Puffin?"

The major flushed. "Don't know what you're talking about, Twit."

"Overheard you telling Callie all about your exploits just yesterday."

The major straightened his tie and glanced around the patio. "Yes, excellent woman. Highly intelligent. Hoped she might ... you know ... be in the vicinity?"

"Got a crush on her have you, Puffin?" asked Lord Featherington-Twit.

Major Puffin cleared his throat. "Certainly not. Not often such a fine figure of a woman comes to these parts. Any red-blooded male, worth his salt would be crazy not to want to ... well you know ... amazing woman."

Aidan loosened his collar. "Did he say 'fine figure of a woman'?"

Lissy smiled. "I believe that's *exactly* what he said."

"Of course, conversation implies you *both* talk," said Basil. "Sounded like a one-way street to me,

Puffin. No wonder Callie left. Bored the woman silly."

Major Puffin rose to his feet. "I take offense to that remark, sir. At least I know one end of a rifle from the other."

Featherington-Twit narrowed his eyes. "Don't make me hurt you, Puffin."

"Hurt me? Hurt me? I'll tell you, sir, I captained the Harrow rugger team from 1955 to 1956."

Featherington-Twit shrugged off his jacket. "And that's supposed to scare me is it, Puffin? I'll have you know you're talking to Oxford's 1957 heavyweight champion."

Puffin threw his blazer at Cagney, smacking her neatly in the eye with a gold button. Immediately the men raised their fists and started to bob and weave like two senior citizens having some kind of vertical fit.

Sensing the tension, Balmoral snapped hold of Featherington-Twit's pant leg, her teeth snarling, her short stubby tail flapping like an out of control metronome.

"Control your beast, Puffin." The lord shook his leg, as the wiry mutt clung on for dear life.

Major Puffin ducked a particularly vicious right hook. "Soon as you apologize."

"Boys, boys!" Henri raised a hand in protest, but her heart wasn't in it.

Featherington-Twit tried desperately to free his leg from Balmoral. "Release me, you brute." But Balmoral was having way too much fun.

Suddenly, Baskerville threw back his head and yowled before charging towards Windsor and Buckingham. The two dogs careened across the patio, followed by Baskerville's long strides.

Lissy hopped onto the balustrade. Tess bounded onto her chair. They gaped as Baskerville chased the two dogs round and round the table. Baskerville stood at least a foot taller than the corgis and weighed significantly more, but the table was the smaller dogs' friend as they weaved in and out of its legs.

An ice-cold gust of wind whipped across the patio. Aidan peeked up in time to see the pretty young maid with red hair hurry back into the castle.

With any luck she was off to fetch Carrington. Someone needed to stop the two men before someone got hurt and, right now, Carrington seemed the best bet.

"Erm! Excuse me, major. But I think Baskerville is about to eat Windsor," said Tess.

However, Major Puffin and Lord Featherington-Twit were too busy circling each other like boxers in a ring to notice. Without warning, Puffin lurched towards Featherington-Twit. The lord caught his foe in a headlock and the two teetered back and forth across the patio in some strange tug-of-war. Goodness knows how long it would have gone on if Lissy hadn't screamed.

The two men came to an abrupt stop. Both Featherington-Twit and Puffin swiveled towards Lissy. Standing on top of the balustrade, she pointed towards Henri.

As the two men shuffled forward to get a better view, they were just in time to see Henri slip down her chair and slide under the table.

*

✳

*

18

Bumble Bottom

The boxing match came to a halt as Featherington-Twit checked Henri for injuries, before hoisting his wife to her feet. Henri insisted everyone stop fussing. Major Puffin and his dogs departed, and Carrington declared dinner well and truly ready.

Dinner consisted of the best savory pie Tess had ever tasted and it was all Olivia could do to stop her sister having fourths. Dinner consumed, Lord Featherington-Twit suggested the cousins take a walk into the village and enjoy the long summer evening. Thinking he might want some time alone with Henri, the cousins agreed, and, following Lord Featherington-Twit's directions, the five headed across the lawn, past the cows and into the forest.

Tess pointed at a wooden signpost with a little walking man etched into one of the arms. "Look, it's a 'T' for Tess."

"It's the public footpath Henri told us about," said Aidan. "We follow this and we should reach the village."

"Do you think Henri will be okay?" asked Lissy.

"She's fine," said Olivia. "Lord F-T said she's been having sleeping problems and sometimes she drifts off."

Twenty minutes later, the cousins emerged from a narrow, overgrown lane onto the main street of Bumble Bottom. An old-fashioned red phone box stood marking the secret passageway, a matching red mailbox by its side.

Lissy examined the front of the squat red box. "Look Tess, it has Lilibet's crest on the front."

Tess grinned. "Wow! Being queen definitely has its perks."

The cousins continued along the High Street. There was a butchers and a bakery but, to Tess' dismay, no candlestick shop. A small grocery store acted as a post office, and next to it stood an antique store.

Tess darted across the road and pressed her nose against the bakery window. The sign above read 'Upper Crust'. Tess slipped inside, emerging two minutes later with a brown paper bag that showed the distinct signs of grease.

Cagney shook her head. "You cannot *possibly* be hungry."

Tess licked a sticky finger. "Not anymore."

Cagney eyed Tess' stick-thin frame. She wondered, for the hundredth time, where Tess put all that food. She decided Tess must have a hollow leg, maybe even two.

Tess skipped across the street and peered into the window of the antique store. "Oooh, look at this."

Olivia squinted over her shoulder. "What, the doll?"

Tess nodded. "Aha. It's a Cindy doll. Like an English Barbie, but you can tell she's English because—"

"She's got crooked teeth?" suggested Cagney.

Tess wrinkled her nose. "I was *going* to say because she's sophis ... sopha ... so—"

"Sophisticated," suggested Lissy, coming to the rescue.

"That's the word," said Tess, cheerfully.

"Let's go take a look," said Aidan, spying a large bookcase at the rear of the store.

"Absolutely not ..." but Cagney's words were lost, as Tess barged through the door.

The cousins trudged inside. From dolls to dishes, tables to tea-sets, the store overflowed with anything and everything English. Aidan headed straight for the bookcase, Tess towards various sized dolls. Cagney spied brightly colored clothes hanging from a rack, and Lissy inspected the jewels sparkling in an old fashioned jewelry cabinet.

Olivia traipsed towards the back of the store and slumped into an overstuffed armchair. Shopping was *not* her thing. She closed her eyes and wondered if Grandma was having fun. Of *course* she was having fun. Grandma was in London, and London was far more interesting than Bumble Bottom. Sure, the village was cute in a Christmas card kind of way, but Olivia didn't want cute. Olivia wanted adventure, and there was about as much chance of adventure here as Cagney developing a passion for rock climbing.

Her thoughts were interrupted by a voice coming from behind a curtain. The voice was familiar. Olivia scratched her head. What was the likelihood of knowing someone in an antique store in the middle of nowhere? Pretty slim. Olivia wasn't an eavesdropper, but the familiarity of the voice drew her in, and pretty soon she realized she was listening to someone's conversation.

"It's too dangerous, I tell ya. As long as you don't go losing your 'ead, we'll be scott free."

There was a muffled reply before the familiar voice spoke again. "Can't it wait? Alright then, same time, same place. But I don't like it. I don't like it one little bit. I don't care how cold he is, nor how 'ungry. He can bleedin' lump it."

Olivia stopped listening and thought how much the man behind the curtain sounded like Billy. However, when the man appeared he looked nothing like Billy and sounded nothing like him either.

"Well, hello!" said the man, a warm smile on his face.

The man was tall, well-built and dressed in white. He reminded Olivia of a film star her mom liked, but with auburn hair and far bluer eyes. The man strode behind the counter and produced a large wooden bat. It was wider and flatter than a baseball bat and had red tape at one end. He slung it over his shoulder and trotted towards Olivia.

Leaning down, he hoisted Olivia from the chair. "Sorry," he said, with a grin, herding Olivia towards the exit, "but Odds and Ends is closed and the Pickled Herrings wait for no man."

Olivia frowned.

"Yes, the Googly Gherkin's going to thrash those Limpley Eleven. At least, I hope we will. Last year we took a walloping! But I have high hopes."

By this time the others had stopped browsing and were watching intently.

Cagney stuffed a clown costume back onto the rack of clothes and hurried towards the door. She was rewarded with a gleaming smile.

The man shepherded the five onto the street before turning to lock the store.

"I'm so dreadfully sorry, but if you come back tomorrow, you can browse more then."

"But," Olivia pointed towards the window, "what about the friend you were talking to?"

"I know!" The man strolled down the street, shaking his bat in the air. "They'll be furious."

Olivia turned to Cagney, but she was gawking after the man, a dreamy expression on her face.

"Did you understand any of that?" asked Olivia.

Aidan snapped his fingers in front of his sister's face. "Something about eleven gherkins?"

"But what did he mean?" Olivia turned back to the store and squinted through the glass. She could see no one. Maybe there was a back exit. Surely the owner wouldn't have locked the person he was talking to in the store?

Aidan shrugged. "I have absolutely no idea."

"Aidan! Look!" Lissy pointed towards him.

"What?" Aidan wheeled around, brushing his shoulders. "It's not a spider, is it?"

"No! You've still got the book you were reading," explained Lissy.

Aidan glanced down. Sure enough, in his hand lay a small volume of English verse. He turned to flag down the Googly Gherkin man, but he had already disappeared behind the butcher's shop.

"Come on," said Aidan. "Maybe we can catch him."

Suddenly, Aidan felt a movement on his shoulder. *Yikes, maybe it was a spider after all.* He reached up to brush the insect away but instead his hand touched something cold. Something hairy. Something human.

19

Potty Potts

Aidan jerked his head towards whatever landed on his shoulder. Grasping his Ralph Lauren polo shirt were the dirtiest, grimiest fingernails he'd ever seen. The grip was impressive and so was the smell. Only once had Aidan seen a hand even half as dirty, and Olivia had worked for hours to achieve it.

Aidan's eyes traveled up the hand and along a filthy sleeve. Peeping over his shoulder stood a solid man with a bedraggled face and bushy gray hair bulging from beneath a floppy hat.

Aidan turned towards Olivia for help, but she and the others were gazing through the window. *Great, Olivia had to choose now to develop an interest in shopping.*

The man stared at Aidan, his brows knitted, his mouth a tight scowl. Aidan tried to back away, but the man's hold was tight and Aidan didn't want to rip his shirt; it was his favorite.

Who was this guy? Surely not the police. Aidan dismissed such thoughts. This might be a tiny village, but surely the policemen didn't look like this. Besides, he hadn't actually stolen the book of poetry, just temporarily possessed it.

Eventually one of the girls would turn. Aidan decided to stay put until they did. He mustered a smile. From behind his scraggly beard, the man smiled back.

Finally, Olivia turned and hurried towards them. "Hey, what's going on?"

Aidan relaxed. He was pretty sure if the situation demanded it, Olivia could 'take' the stranger. But, to be honest, the man didn't seem as menacing as before.

"Erm!" said Aidan, finding his voice. "I think we have a slight misunderstanding about the book."

"Book!" said the man, pointing.

"You want it?" asked Aidan.

By now the others had stopped browsing, and three of the four had gathered around Aidan for support. Cagney was obviously offering support from a distance, thought Aidan, watching his sister back into the shop doorway.

Released from his clutches, Aidan finally got a good view of the stranger. The man was wrapped in a gray raincoat tied with string and upon his feet the muddiest wellies Aidan had ever had the misfortune to see.

The man continued to point at the book. "Book," he repeated, more urgently.

Tess plucked the book of poetry from Aidan's hands and offered it to the man. "Here, *you* have it." She smiled at the stranger. "And take these too." She held out the scrunched up pastry bag in her other hand. The man seemed confused, but slowly reached forward and snatched the offerings before turning and shuffling down the street.

"Come on," said Aidan. "Let's go find Googly and explain we need to pay for a book."

Before them sprawled the village green, a church spire rising in the distance. To the left sat a duck pond and beyond it a white building with black stripes leaning drunkenly into the lane. The grass lay surrounded by brightly colored cottages, white picket fences and tiny parked cars.

"Where is everyone?" Lissy glanced at her watch. She was still on Texas time; she did a quick calculation and frowned. "Surely people don't go to bed this early in the country?"

Suddenly a loud cheer erupted as a stream of men came bounding from the black and white building, heading towards the village green.

As the cousins approached they saw several picnic benches hidden behind a hedge. Sitting on the benches were several men and women, clapping as each man trotted by.

"What's going on?" asked Tess.

A young woman with long, highlighted hair appeared. Wearing a mini skirt, plunging halterneck and heels Cagney could only dream of walking in, she draped an arm around Tess' shoulder. "That's the cricket team from the Pickled Herring."

"But what's a pickled herring?" asked Olivia.

"It's the pub in our neighboring village, Limpley-under-Water. And here are our lot." Whistles and clapping greeted more men as they ambled across the cobblestones.

"Come on, Googly Gherkins," the woman cried.

Tess recognized the antique store owner's auburn hair as he strode down the steps, saluting the cousins with his cricket bat.

"So, that's what he was talking about," said Olivia. "Cricket."

"Who is he?" asked Cagney, nonchalantly, trying not to stare.

The woman smiled. "That's the owner of Odds and Ends. Our resident village hunk, Mister Rupert Smythe."

Olivia snorted, *what kind of name was Rupert? Come to think of it, what kind of name was Smythe?* But Cagney obviously had no such worries.

"Ah, so that makes sense of the Odds and Ends and Pickled Herrings," said Aidan. "Now I just want to know what a Googly Gherkin is?"

The woman in heels jabbed a finger towards a wooden sign hanging above the door. "A Googly Gherkin? Why, that would be my pub."

20

Haunted

The cousins ordered a round of lemonade and several bags of chips called Hula Hoops. Sitting on picnic benches, they watched as each man strolled onto the lawn to bat.

Tess quickly mimicked every schoolchild in England by sticking the Hula Hoops on her fingers and munching them off bite by bite. Finally, Tess tore her attention away from her salt and vinegar fingers. "I hear jingle bells."

"And I see dead people," said Cagney, popping the last Hula Hoop in her mouth.

"No, really, I do."

Cagney listened. Sure enough, the faint sound of bells could be heard, and they were getting louder.

Tess clambered to her feet. "It's Santa!"

However, instead of being greeted by eight tiny reindeer, Tess was treated to twelve humongous men skipping from behind the hedge. The men were dressed identically, in straw hats, white billowing shirts, jewel-colored vests and pants ending in a flourish at the knee. Jingling from the knees down were tiny bells, and in their hands they clutched wooden sticks.

Cagney grabbed her camera. "This village just gets better and better."

"They're Morris Men," said Lissy. "I remember reading about them on Spider."

"But why are they dressed like ..." Tess couldn't think of an appropriate word. Besides, she was upset the bells hadn't produced so much as an elf.

"That's what Morris Dancers wear. They visit villages and dance traditional folk dances. I think it's rather quaint," said Lissy.

"But why?" said Cagney. "Why would anyone go out dressed like *that*?"

"I don't know," replied Lissy. "Maybe they're just happy."

"That's one word for them." Olivia eyed the men with suspicion. "You'd get your behind kicked if you walked down the street like that in Texas."

The cousins watched the men form lines and begin the strangest dance they'd ever seen. Bashing sticks and yelling for joy, the men weaved in and out of each other, skipping and linking arms.

"Good grief," said Cagney, "they're ..."

"Frolicking," said Olivia.

"Yeah," said Cagney, "and in public."

"It's like *Chitty Chitty Bang Bang*," said Tess.

Aidan nodded. It was his favorite movie and, in this quaint village, with these peculiarly dressed dancers, Aidan felt like he was starring in his very own musical.

"Look!" said Olivia, who could only take so much skipping in one day.

Peeking out from behind the hedge stood the man with the book. He studied the dancers suspiciously. Cautiously, he edged his way around the hedge, before dashing into the middle of the dance troop.

Olivia grinned. "That's more like it."

The man grabbed one of the wooden sticks and leapt into the air.

Lissy gasped, but the Morris Men were obviously used to such interruptions and jingled their bells in delight. The patrons at the picnic tables let out a roar of approval, as the man twirled his way through the crowd, flinging himself and his ancient raincoat in and out of spectators.

"I guess they must know him," said Aidan.

"That's Potty Potts," said a voice.

Aidan spun around in time to see the owner of the Googly Gherkin wobble towards them.

"D'you know him?" asked Cagney.

"Course! He's harmless enough. Just the local tramp. Potts has lived in Bumble Bottom all his life. Lives in a caravan down Blackberry Lane. No one really takes any notice of him. Keeps to himself, mainly. But he does love to dance."

"You don't say." Cagney watched as Potts linked arms with an unsuspecting Morris Man and spun him in a circle.

"That must be the man Lord Featherington-Twit talked about earlier," said Lissy.

"You're staying with the Twits, are you? You must be Callie's grandchildren." The pub owner placed her glass on the table and attempted to raise her leg over the bench seat. "'Ere, shift up. Name's Sally, by the way."

It used to come as a surprise when complete strangers announced they knew their grandma. By now the cousins were used to it.

"Tell us whatcha got up to in London."

Cagney told Sally about their time in the city, their trip to the Tower and their meeting with the queen.

"Well, blow me down," said Sally, when Cagney finally drew breath. "You do seem to have an 'abit of getting in trouble."

"So we've been told," said Tess.

"Not much chance of getting in trouble here though," said Olivia.

"Ooh," said Sally. "Don't you be putting down village life. Lots a things go on here likes you'd never find in the big city."

"Like what?" asked Cagney.

"Well, first off, we have our own anchoress."

"Like on a ship?" asked Tess.

"No, there be no ships 'round these parts. An anchoress is someone who's bricked into the wall of a church." Sally pointed towards the steeple on the far side of the green.

Lissy looked distraught. "Shouldn't someone get her out?"

Sally twirled an enormous gold earring. "She's not there anymore, silly. That was back in the fourteenth century."

"But how did she eat and you know ..." Lissy trailed off.

"Poop!" said Tess. "Where did she go to the restroom?"

Sally laughed. "There's a small opening in the side of the wall, large enough to pass food and, you know ... stuff, in and out. The village took turns feeding her and, in return, the anchoress spent her days praying for them."

"Probably praying someone would let her out," said Aidan, who was claustrophobic and could think of few things worse.

"It was completely voluntary," replied Sally. "They didn't just brick her in coz she'd been a bit naughty or anything."

Lissy shook her head and imagined what it would be like to say goodbye to your family and willingly be entombed in the side of a church. Lissy gulped. It sounded barbaric.

"Voluntary or not, that churchyard gives me the collywobbles. It was all right when I was a kid; used it as a cut-through to get to the brook. But no one goes near it now, 'specially at night. Said to be haunted, it is." Sally lowered her voice. "Often, when I'm closing on a Friday, I'll see a shadow flit across the church wall."

Lissy paled, Tess shivered and Aidan felt goose bumps rise along his arm.

"Course, the Googly Gherkin's haunted as well, you know. Every so often I'll feel a strange draft. Recently stuff's gone missing. Not to mention sounds coming from places where sounds just shouldn't be. Yep, all kinds of stories about this village I could be telling you."

Olivia shrugged. She didn't believe in ghosts. She didn't believe in anything unless she'd seen it with her own eyes.

Sally took a sip of her drink. "Also, I've heard it said our Googly Gherkin's one of the coaching inns used by Dick Turpin."

"Who's Dick Turpin?" asked Aidan, happy to change the subject away from ghosts.

"Oh, I know," said Lissy. "He was a highwayman in the eighteenth century. He used to rob stage coaches."

"Just like Robin Hood?" asked Tess.

"Kind of," said Sally. "Except dear old Dick didn't have any intention of giving to the poor. Kept the lot for himself. A very wealthy man, was our Dick. Course, they hanged him in the end."

"Hanged who?" said a rough voice.

Behind Sally stood a tall, slim man, with a buzz cut. He would have been good looking if he'd smiled, thought Lissy.

Sally spun around and burst out laughing. "You scared the life out of me, Nick Ratcliffe."

"I'll be doing more than that if you don't get yourself inside, woman. Bar's packed and you're sitting out here chatting with a bunch of kids."

Sally took another sip of her drink. "These are Callie's grandchildren."

Nick's cold eyes glanced over the cousins. "I don't care who they are. Get inside and make yourself useful."

Olivia scowled. This was not how a man should speak to his girlfriend. She saw Aidan shuffle uncomfortably. He wasn't liking it either. Olivia's thoughts were interrupted by the owner of the antique store approaching.

Rupert's face was flushed and his smile broad. "Hey, Sally. Nick!"

Nick mumbled something uncharitable and glared as Rupert headed into the pub.

Sally watched Rupert's retreating back. Catching Nick's scowl, she looked away with a self-conscious laugh. "I was telling them about the Googly Gherkin being haunted. About those sounds and all that food going missing."

Nick scowled. "You're imagining things. Drank too much cider."

Sally peered at her half empty glass. "He might be right. But they sounded pretty real to me. Maybe Dick Turpin's haunting us after all."

"Dick Turpin came nowhere near this village. It's just an old wives tale," said Nick, his face flushed.

"Oh!" said Sally, shrugging. "History never was my strong point."

Nick seemed even more furious. "Are you going to stand around all day, Sally Bishop, or am I gonna have to serve the entire village by me self?"

"Keep your hair on." Sally struggled to her feet, unfolding herself from the clutches of the bench. But the picnic table wasn't releasing her so easily. The publican's shoe caught on a cobblestone and Sally went down in a heap.

Three men in uniform strode from around the hedge. Walking in unison they headed towards the picnic tables.

On seeing Sally flat on her back, the youngest rushed forward. He grasped the barmaid under the arms and hauled her to her feet.

"A gentleman. How rare." Sally gave Nick a sarcastic glance.

"The name's Pickle, ma'am. P.C. Pickle."

Sally did her best to hide her smile.

The largest of the men stepped forward. His voice was soft, deep and sounded like it was used to getting its own way.

"Excuse me, *sir*, but would you happen to be Nick Ratcliffe?"

Nick eyed the older man suspiciously. "Who's asking?"

Olivia studied the imposing newcomer, suddenly realizing he was the first person in the village she'd seen, other than her and Tess, who wasn't white.

The man fished in his breast pocket and pulled out his ID. His mouth smiled, his eyes did not. "Detective Inspector Watts of the Metropolitan Police. If we could have a moment, sir."

21

Trouble

*S*ally plopped onto the picnic bench. "Oh, lawd!"

Nick's face seemed fit to burst. "I've been over this a dozen times with the local plod."

"Yes, sir," said D.I. Watts, running steely brown eyes over Nick. "But we are *not* the local plod, are we?"

P.C. Pickle stepped forward and nodded towards the pub. "How about somewhere more private to talk, Mr. Ratcliffe?"

Nick scowled. "I'm fine right 'ere."

There was silence. The Morris Men stopped jingling, the patrons quit drinking. Even the cricketers ceased cricketing.

"I haven't seen him, all right?" Nick looked as uncomfortable as a pig on pogo stick. "And yes, if he contacts me I will be sure to let you know just as fast as me fingers can dial 999."

Inspector Watts' eyebrows rose. "Mr. Ratcliffe, are you expecting us to believe your brother has yet to contact you since getting out of Her Majesty's Prison? It's been a full two weeks, son."

Nick went scarlet. Clenching his teeth, his words came out in a hiss. "I guess, when you've been locked up at Her Majesty's pleasure for five years, it takes the closeness out of a relationship."

The two younger policemen exchanged glances. D.I. Watts' gaze did not leave Nick's face.

"You guys just don't get it, do you? Just coz my no good brother decides to nick a few trinkets, doesn't mean I'm up to somefing."

Inspector Watts' lips stretched into a thin line. "Young man, I would not exactly be calling them *trinkets*. Gary Ratcliffe is a hardened criminal."

P.C. Pickle opened his notebook and cleared his throat. "He is, and I quote, 'The brains behind the opal fiasco. The mastermind behind the disappearance of Lady Featherington-Twits' tiara.' And finally, justice seems to have been served when he was caught red-handed in the Richmond ruby riot."

"Lady Featherington-Twit owns a tiara?" gasped Tess.

P.C. Pickle pursed his lips. "Not any more, she don't."

Nick finally lost his cool. "Just coz my brother's a crook *doesn't* mean you have the right to harass me." And with that, he stormed into the Googly Gherkin.

The policemen followed. The Morris Men jingled off and the patrons resumed their chatter.

"Whoa!" said Aidan. "Talk about uncomfortable."

Sally downed the rest of her drink. "He's not bad, is my Nick. He's just no darn good. But since his brother got out of prison, and with the crown jewels going missing. Well, the village has been swarming with coppers ever since it hit the papers. They just won't leave him alone."

Olivia caught Aidan's eye. Things were falling into place. No wonder Grandma visited Bumble

Bottom, especially if Lady F-T had lost a valuable piece of headgear.

"Nick keeps telling them he's not heard from Gary, but they won't believe him." Sally peeped over her shoulder and lowered her voice. "I only saw Gary once. Not the nicest man I've ever met, always smelled of pickles."

"So why *do* they keep questioning Nick? I mean, if he's completely innocent," asked Lissy.

"Well." Sally cleared her throat. "I wouldn't say he was *completely* innocent. He's been in and out the nick a few times." Sally took in Lissy's blank face. "Been in prison. Petty stuff. But he's a reformed character, he is. He's been a good lad, fixing up the guest rooms and doing all kinds of odd jobs. Besides, he's promised he'll stay on the straight and narrow."

"And you believe him?" asked Aidan.

Sally took a deep breath. "I'm trying to."

22

The Anchoress

Sally left and the cousins finished their snacks. Olivia drained her drink. "Anyone want to go see where the anchoress was holed in?"

Lissy shuddered. "No! I don't."

Olivia glanced around expectantly. "No one?" She shrugged. "All right. You guys stay here. Aidan and I will go."

Aidan choked on a Hula Hoop. "I don't want to go."

"You're going to let your favorite cousin wander around a haunted graveyard by herself?"

"Yes and no."

"Well, which is it?" asked Olivia.

"Yes, I'm going to let you wander around a haunted graveyard, and no, you're not my favorite cousin."

Olivia grinned. "Well, if *I'm* not, who is?"

Aidan swallowed. "The ones *not* asking me to walk around a haunted graveyard."

Olivia turned and headed across the village green towards the spire. The church sat at the far end of the village, a couple of hundred yards away from the pub with an obelisk perched by its entryway.

Olivia had learned from her dad about the two World Wars fought in the last century. She looked closely and realized this must be a war memorial. Olivia inspected the names and dates etched in stone. She shook her head. There were way too many names - some of the young men just a few years older than Aidan.

She kept walking until she reached the stone wall surrounding the churchyard. Sally could talk all she wanted about ghosts and hauntings, but Olivia wasn't scared. She wasn't scared of anything. Well, hardly anything. Slowly, she passed through a swing gate and headed towards the church. Sally had said you could still see where the anchoress had been entombed along the north wall near an ancient yew tree.

Olivia had no idea which way was north. Come to think of it, she had no idea what a yew tree looked like either. Spotting a humongous tree to her left she decided to head that way and wandered down the overgrown path. Amazingly, there was still enough light to see. The summer days were far longer in England than in Texas, that was for sure.

As she passed the sprawling tree she spied the outline of an archway etched on the side of the church. On it rested a small plaque. Olivia trotted towards it and stood on tiptoes trying to read. It was no good; the plaque was hung too high.

To her right stood a rectangular stone tomb. Maybe if she climbed on top and leaned over she could get a better view. *Were you allowed to climb on graves?* Olivia scratched her head. She didn't want to be disrespectful. She was just contemplating this dilemma when a shadow flitted across the archway.

Olivia ducked behind the tomb. The shadow grew longer. Good grief, what was she thinking?

Why had she come to a graveyard alone? Why hadn't she listened to Sally about ghosts and ghouls and, hang on, she recognized that voice. It was familiar. It was the same voice she'd heard behind the curtain at Odds and Ends.

Olivia stuck her head out from behind the grave. A man stood silhouetted by the feeble streetlight. He was talking to somebody, but dusk was now turning to dark and, for the life of her, Olivia couldn't see where or who the other person was.

The voices became louder - agitated. Definitely not ghosts. Olivia rolled her eyes. Of course they weren't ghosts. Ghosts didn't exist. But why were these people meeting in the graveyard? Sally had said the entire village wouldn't go into the churchyard after dark. Well, obviously two people did - three, if you counted her.

A few words drifted towards her. Hungry …. scared … plod … and what the heck was a manhole cover? She tried to make sense of the words, but the men were too far away to hear more. Suddenly, Olivia heard another voice: an American voice. The men heard it at the same time and took off across the graveyard. Speeding past the street lamp Olivia spied a flash of auburn hair, as the men fled into the night.

23

Don't Do It Olivia!

Olivia popped up from behind the grave and bounded towards her cousin. Aidan had got as far as the yew tree and, by the expression on his face, wasn't going any farther.

"Come on," said Aidan, glancing around. "It's getting dark."

Olivia decided not to say anything about Rupert and the mystery man from behind the curtain. Aidan had obviously not seen them and she wasn't exactly sure what to say, although she would ask him to explain some of those words later.

They raced across the village green. Aidan was right, it *had* grown dark. The others were waiting for them, and quickly they all headed along the High Street before traipsing down the hidden lane.

Aidan wished he'd brought his flashlight. It wasn't far to the castle, but the woods filtered out any moonlight and twice he'd tripped on a log. He didn't even want to think about what he'd stepped in. There'd been a lot of dogs in these woods during the day and Aidan had a good idea what they'd been doing.

"So, what do you think of Nick Ratcliffe?" asked Olivia.

"He's hiding something," said Lissy.

Aidan nodded. "I agree. But what?"

"A bunch of tiaras. That's what," said Cagney.

Finally the lights of Castle Featherington-Twit came into view. The cousins emerged from the forest and onto the grass. Aidan was just about to inspect his new loafers when, without warning, Tess leapt behind him.

"Good grief," cried Cagney, "what is it?"

Tess pointed towards the castle. In the dark, several shapes moved across the lawn.

"Don't be such a wuss," said Olivia. "They're just..." Olivia squinted. "Actually, I don't know *what* they are."

"They're skunks!" Tess had excellent eyesight and nobody doubted her.

Cagney started to hyperventilate. "What are you going to do?"

Having once been skunked, Aidan had no intention of it happening again. "We need to get to the castle as quickly as we can."

"They're fast little critters." Cagney shoved Olivia forward. "Why don't you go first?"

"See if they're friendly," said Lissy.

Olivia rolled her eyes. She didn't want to get skunked either, but would rather smell like a sewer than admit it. She sidled around the edge of the woods. "Nice skunky, skunky, skunk," she murmured. Olivia was known for her love of animals, but even she wasn't crazy enough to startle a skunk. Besides, these were the biggest skunks she'd ever seen; huge, in fact.

"Not skunks!" came a whisper through the night.

Olivia spun around to find Potts, the tramp from the village, standing behind her.

"Badgers," he mumbled. "No skunks in England."

"Will they hurt me?" asked Olivia, slightly unnerved by Potts' sudden appearance.

"Not unless you give 'em cause." And with that, he disappeared into the woods.

Olivia scanned the grounds. The others were huddled against the tree line, their eyes glued towards the castle. They hadn't seen the tramp emerge from the shadows. It was time to have some fun. Olivia strode towards the badgers.

Lissy was the first to see her. "Olivia! Get back!"

Olivia kept walking. "You know, skunks have a bad reputation. I think these ones are friendly."

"Are you nuts?" cried Cagney. "Don't you remember how gross Aidan smelled? Dad made him sleep in the garden for a whole week."

"Two," sighed Aidan.

"And he still stunk even then. Plus, the tomato juice dad used to counteract the smell made his hair turn orange." Cagney had thoroughly enjoyed those two weeks and had documented Aidan's change in hair color through a zoom lens.

Olivia didn't break stride.

Lissy shut her eyes. "Thank goodness she's not sleeping in my room."

"Yes, but she's sleeping in mine," wailed Tess. "Don't do it, Olivia! Think of your sister."

Olivia grinned. She was now within a few feet of the badgers. On closer inspection she couldn't believe she'd thought they were skunks. For sure, they had white stripes, but they were much plumper than any skunk Olivia had ever seen and kind of cuddly looking. Olivia wondered if she could take one back to Texas as a pet.

Olivia made a shooing motion. "Scram! Get out of here."

The badgers turned and waddled across the lawn straight towards the others.

"They're coming!" screamed Lissy.

"Run for it!" cried Aidan.

"Every woman for herself," yelled Cagney, pushing her cousins aside and hurtling into the night.

The others needed no encouragement. Within seconds they had scattered in four directions.

The badgers, however, had only one direction in mind and subsequently chased only one cousin. The loudest.

"Get it away! Get it away," yelled Cagney, as she tore across the grass. However, her screams seemed to encourage them, as five badgers lumbered in pursuit.

It was hard to run in the dark, especially in the footwear Cagney had chosen. If she could only get to the castle. Surely they wouldn't follow her into the castle? Cagney glanced around. She couldn't believe it. The darn things were gaining on her. Suddenly, her ankle turned and Cagney landed belly first on the grass.

Cagney closed her eyes and tried not to inhale. She also tried not to think about what she'd landed in. Surely not? It was warm. It was wet and it smelled - good grief did it smell. Cagney remembered the cows she'd passed earlier and could have cried.

Cagney's fingers inched their way out of the gloop, trying to find a dry spot of grass. She wanted

more than anything to brush her hair off her face -
but daren't.

Olivia trotted up behind her. "It's okay, Cagney.
They're badgers. They're harmless."

Cagney raised her head. Forgetting what dripped
off her fingers, she pushed a clump of hair from her
eyes. It was the straw that broke the Texan's back.

Cagney leapt to her feet and stormed towards
her cousin.

Olivia may have been reckless, but she was not
stupid. She straightened up and ran.

*
* *

24

Things that go Bump in the Night

Cagney plodded around the moat, over the drawbridge and into the courtyard. Olivia had vanished completely and the others, having wisely decided to give her some space, could just be made out disappearing through the castle's medieval door.

Save for a couple of lights ablaze on the second floor, the castle was cloaked in darkness. Lord Featherington-Twit had not set a time for them to return, and Cagney spared a thought for Carrington, hoping they weren't keeping him awake. Being on American time had its advantages, but not to those who were trying to get to sleep at a decent hour.

Sticky, muddy and encrusted in lord knew what, Cagney hobbled across the courtyard. Reaching the door, she was about to grasp the handle when the door creaked open.

Cagney had barely stepped inside when a gust of cold air swept over the moat causing the door to slam shut. A shiver pierced her spine as Cagney remembered the tale of the white lady. *Great. Just great.*

Luckily, in the dim light, Cagney could make out the young maid with hair as red as blood standing at the end of the corridor. Thank goodness someone was still up. The castle was a warren of twists and turns and Cagney didn't have a good sense of direction; she might as well be asked to find Atlantis as to find the south wing. Following the maid, Cagney navigated her way through the corridors. Fortunately for Olivia, by the time she got to her room, Cagney was too exhausted to deal with her cousin.

The silence was broken by the hoot of an owl and the squeak of a floorboard as something padded down the corridor.

Cagney had showered and changed and now slept flat on her back. Lissy lay beside her, a pillow pulled tight around her curls. Slowly the handle on the door turned. Bit by bit the door eased open.

Cagney bolted upright. "What was that?" Fumbling for her glasses, she peered into the darkness, filled her lungs and released a blood-curdling scream.

Olivia shook the feet lying on the pillow next to her. "Tess, did you hear that?"

Tess opened an eye. "Hear what?"

"A—" Olivia was about to say 'scream' but was interrupted by the door bursting open and Cagney and Lissy tumbling through it.

Cagney's face was pale, her hair electrified. "I saw a … a …"

Lissy folded her arms and huffed. "She saw the White Lady."

"Ooooh! Was she pretty?" asked Tess.

Cagney toppled onto the end of the bed. "I saw a ghost, and all you ask is, 'was she pretty'?"

"Oooh, I bet she was." Tess scrambled to a sitting position. "With a long white dress, her pale blonde hair flowing down her back."

"She was terrifying! I mean, ghosts shouldn't be allowed to creep in and out of people's bedrooms in the middle of the night. They could seriously scare someone."

Lissy rolled her eyes. "I think that's the point."

Olivia sank into her pillow and closed her eyes. "You don't *believe* in ghosts, remember?"

Goose bumps scooted up Cagney's arms causing her to shiver. "I do now."

*
*   *
*

25

Robbery

Tess' pajama-clad bottom arched into the air as the morning sunlight fell across the bed. Tess was a fidgety sleeper who could sleep through anything. Olivia could *not* sleep through anything, especially when that 'thing' was Tess.

Olivia focused on a movement near the doorway. She rubbed the sleep from her eyes and stretched. Slowly, the door creaked open. Olivia felt her breath catch as a pale hand slithered around the door. The hand was followed by a head, hovering towards the top of the door. The head turned and smiled, and Olivia let go of her breath.

"Bad news, I'm afraid," said Lady Featherington-Twit, entering the room.

Olivia gave Tess a not-so-gentle kick, and when that failed, pulled a toe. Tess snorted and rolled over. Olivia gave up. "What happened?"

"It's not so much *what's* happening as what's *not* happening."

"Erm ..." said Olivia, confused.

"Blasted plumbing's given up the ghost. Plumber's on his way. Mind you, British workmen." Lady Featherington-Twit rolled her eyes. "Could be Christmas before we take a bath."

"Do you want us to leave? I mean, we could go back to London. You know, get out your way." Olivia grinned and then remembered the Featherington-Twits plumbing was broken and attempted a more somber expression.

"No need, no need. Booked us all into the Googly Gherkin for a couple of nights. Turns out they have a few rooms to let and Sally's an absolute dear. Although I've no idea what she sees in that Ratcliffe fellow."

"Yeah," said Olivia. "Actually, the police were there last night."

"No surprise there," said Lady Featherington-Twit. "Anyway, can't leave yet. Village fête starts tomorrow and Basil and I are opening it."

After a hearty breakfast the five decided to stroll down to the village and explore. As they walked, Cagney told Aidan all about her encounter with the White Lady. By now the story contained several ghostly sounds and at least two deathly smells.

"You know, I'm quite enjoying these walks," said Aidan. "I mean, I wouldn't want to do it all the time, but there's a peacefulness here you just don't find in Texas. I'm wondering why I don't walk more at home."

Lissy glanced at Aidan. "I can't be sure, but I'm guessing the temperature being a hundred degrees by noon has something to do with it."

"Not to mention the humidity," said Cagney, who found the English weather most agreeable to her curls.

The cousins emerged onto the High Street and surveyed the scene. To be honest, the scene was rather dull.

Cagney watched a black and white tabby stroll across the road and sighed. "It's really a struggle to know where to go first. I mean, it's all so darn exciting."

At exactly that moment, Sally teetered around the corner. For a woman wearing five-inch heels and a tight satin skirt she could really move. She spotted the cousins and wobbled towards them, grinning broadly. "Hello Callie's grandchildren."

"What's the hurry?" said Aidan, scanning the High Street. "Is there a fire?"

"Better than that." Sally grasped her side and took several deep breaths. "The antique store got broken into last night."

"Oh no!" cried Lissy.

"Yes," continued Sally, smoothing down her cream skirt. "I know. Poor Rupert! Must be devastated. I figured I'd pop along and, you know, help him in his time of need."

"Was anything stolen?" asked Aidan.

"Several things," said Sally. "But the police have already caught the thief."

"They have?" said Lissy. "Wow, that's impressive."

"Amazing, innit? Apparently Potty Potts isn't as harmless as he looks. He was caught red-handed with one of Rupert's books. Silly man didn't even try to hide it." Sally waved goodbye and made her way unsteadily across the street.

There was silence.

Aidan's voice sounded strangled. "What do we do?"

"We should go to the police and tell them," said Lissy. "Straight away. I can't believe that poor man's been locked up and it's all our fault."

Cagney gave her glasses a quick polish. "It's not *my* fault. Besides, I think Aidan should go. He stole the book in the first place."

Aidan glared. "I did *not* steal it."

Cagney smirked. "Did you pay for it?"

Aidan looked sheepish. "I was *going* to pay for it, but then Mr. Smythe shooed us out and I forgot."

"I'm sure they'll take that into consideration when they sentence you," said Cagney. "With any luck you'll be out in a month. Two at the most."

Aidan gulped. He gulped even more when they rounded the corner and saw Inspector Watts descending the steps of the Googly Gherkin.

"Now's your chance." Cagney dragged Aidan towards the policeman.

"Excuse me, sir." Aidan thought his knees were going to buckle.

Inspector Watts slowly nodded his head. "Hello, young man. You'll be Callie's grandson, right?"

Aidan paled. *Great, now Grandma would be dragged into this.* "Erm ... what I mean to ..."

"What my brother is trying to say is, justice has been foiled," said Cagney.

Inspector Watts looked confused, which, under the circumstances, wasn't surprising. He ran his fingers through his black curly hair. "Been what?"

"Foiled, impeded, done wrong. Let me put it this way. You have arrested the wrong man." Cagney shoved Aidan forward. "Here's your culprit."

Aidan got the impression his sister was thoroughly enjoying herself.

Inspector Watts patted Aidan on the shoulder. "Are you talking about Mr. Potter?"

"Yes, sir. You see ..." stammered Aidan.

"Don't you worry, son. It's all been taken care of. He was caught red-handed with several items that Mr. Smythe has positively identified."

"Several?" Cagney's jaw dropped.

"Yes, young lady. Several. Now, if you don't mind. I have a lot to do."

Aidan glanced at Cagney, accusingly.

Cagney scowled. "Hey, don't look at me. Not my fault if Potts is really as Potty as he looks."

*
* *
*

26

Confusion

The cousins strolled past the church, a cheese store whimsically named the Mouse House and several touristy shops selling pictures of a woman being bricked into a wall.

Just as the village came to an end, Aidan finally saw something to make him smile.

Plopped in the middle of a field sat a windowless trailer with the words MOBILE LIBRARY painted in sprawling letters along the side.

Aidan launched himself towards the van and, before anyone could object, bolted up the steps.

Lissy sighed. "I guess it's better than the cheese store."

"There was a cheese store?" asked Tess, swiveling back towards the village.

Olivia grabbed her sister by the scruff of her sparkly tee and herded her up the steps.

The library may have been small, but it was well stocked. Books lay crammed from carpet to ceiling and the warm smell of cinnamon wafted through the air. The smell reminded Tess of the days her mother baked. Although, to be honest, she was also reminded of baking days by the smell of burning.

The librarian was in her forties, with soft brown eyes and hair falling just below her chin. She wore a sweater set, a long flowing skirt and more jewelry than a film star on Oscar night.

Replacing one final book on the shelf, the librarian reached out and shook each of the cousins' hands. "I'm Penelope. Penelope Snodgrass."

Olivia snorted. Lissy shot her a warning look and Olivia grabbed the nearest book. From the look of Olivia's trembling shoulders, plus the fact the book was upside down, Lissy could tell her cousin was far from pulling herself together.

Cagney quickly made the introductions.

"It's not often we have Americans visiting our corner of the world." Penelope paused. "Actually, that's not true. We had a charming lady visit a few days ago. Are you any relation?"

"Probably," said Tess. "Our grandma gets around."

Penelope turned to Tess. "You must hear this all the time, but your accent is adorable."

Tess did *not* hear this all the time. She beamed at Penelope and assumed her strongest Texas drawl, the one she kept for annoying out-of-state relatives.

The others wandered around the trailer. There was a small fiction section and a smaller non-fiction area, but mainly there were books about Bumble Bottom, Limpley-under-Water and other surrounding villages.

Lissy eased a book from the shelves. "Look! This book's about Dick Turpin. That's the highwayman Sally talked about."

Penelope bobbed towards her. "May I?" Her perfectly manicured hands scooped up the book and flipped to chapter twelve. "Here. This will tell you all about Dick Turpin and the time he spent in Bumble Bottom."

Aidan spun to face her. "But he *didn't* spend any time in Bumble Bottom."

Penelope's brow wrinkled. "Who told you that?"

"Nick from the Googly Gherkin," said Tess.

"Nick Ratcliffe?" said Penelope, twisting one of the many rings on her fingers. "What would *he* know? He's not from this neck of the woods."

Lissy let out a squeal. "Listen to this. Turns out Dick Turpin *did* visit Bumble Bottom. He robbed people on the very road leading to the station. He's rumored to have hidden at the Googly Gherkin. It even says there's a secret hiding place used to escape from the authorities. To this day, no-one's been able to find it."

"Fascinating," said Cagney, flipping through the magazine section in hopes of finding the latest *Clamour*. "Dick Turpin in Bumbly Bottom! Well, it just makes your heart go thump, thump - Ow!"

Lissy removed her foot from on top of Cagney's and continued. "It says, not only do they think there's a secret room, but they're pretty sure it contains items he stole. You know, things like watches and purses and money. Lots of money."

Cagney peeked out from behind a copy of Fisherman's Weekly, a grin on her face. "Now that *is* fascinating!"

27

Major Puffin gets Angry

The five wandered back through the village.

"This village is odd," said Cagney. "I'm beginning to think there's some serious inbreeding."

"It does seem that a lot of people were born here," said Aidan. "Lord Featherington-Twit, Sally, Potty Potts."

"Rupert's not from here." Tess twirled around a nearby lamppost. "Sally said so."

"I rest my case," said Cagney. "Only normal one of the lot."

"Nick's not from here either," said Olivia.

"Hmmm! I'm not so sure about him," said Lissy.

"Oooh, look!" Tess pointed at the Cindy doll in the shop window. "It's still there."

They had stopped outside Mr. Smythe's antique store. Lissy pressed her nose to the window and peered into the gloom.

"She's so cute," said Tess. "Look, she even has her own little mini to get to work in."

"Yeah, just wonderful," said Olivia, who was trying to coax a tabby cat out of an alleyway.

Aidan was about to reach the handle when the door jangled open.

Major Puffin stormed into the street wrapped in a tangle of leashes.

Tess stumbled back, tripped over the escaping tabby and landed with a poof on her bottom.

"Oh! My dear girl, I am *so* sorry."

Tess unraveled herself from the leashes and pulled Balmoral off her tummy. "That's okay. She can probably smell the jelly donuts I had for breakfast."

Major Puffin picked up Balmoral and stuffed her under his arm. "Very remiss. Bit topsy-turvy, today. Unusual set of circumstances, though."

Cagney caught Olivia's eye. "What's he talking about?"

Olivia shrugged.

"Major Puffin, are you okay?" Lissy placed a hand on the old man's arm.

He was trembling.

"Thought we were friends," mumbled the major. "Always had tea. Every Friday. I even brought scones with raspberry jam." He rustled a brown paper bag. "Don't know what's got into the man." He glanced back towards the store and took a deep breath. "Hard to know *who* you can trust in this village."

And, without another word, Major Puffin pointed his cane in the direction of the Googly Gherkin and strode down the street.

*
* *
*

28

Argument

The five watched Major Puffin disappear behind the hedge.

"That was strange," said Aidan.

"Very," said Olivia.

"Look," said Lissy. "Isn't that Potts? They must have let him out of jail." She pointed towards a crouching man beneath the hedgerow, his head down, his fingers twisting a piece of string.

"Oooh! Let's go say hi." Tess skipped towards the bedraggled man. "Hello Mr. Potts! Remember us?"

Potty Potts scowled from beneath his filthy hat. His beard, if possible, seemed even more matted, his face hadn't seen a washcloth in a good month of Tuesdays. His eyes darted back and forth along the road. Aidan got the impression that if he'd been standing, Potts would have hightailed it down the road.

Dropping the string, he waved his hands in Tess' face. "Clear off!"

Tess stumbled backwards. "But I ..."

"Go away!" Potts lumbered to his feet and stumbled along the deserted sidewalk.

Aidan laid a hand on Tess' shoulder. "I guess he's in a bad mood. I mean, he *was* thrown in jail; he has every right to be annoyed."

"It's not that." Tess frowned. "There's something wrong."

"You're telling me. Talking to the crazy man is wrong," said Cagney.

"He's harmless." Olivia turned and started up the street. "Come on, let's see if Carrington's delivered our stuff to the Googly Gherkin."

Tess continued to stare. Potty Potts had crossed the road and now leaned against the lamppost opposite Odds and Ends.

"Come on, Tess." Lissy took her cousin's hand. "He didn't mean it."

"Oh, my pink shiny raincoat knows he didn't mean it." Tess followed the others up the street. "But that's what's so weird." She gazed at Potts one last time. "That ... and something else."

Tess' thoughts were interrupted by a noise shattering the village calm like a giant running his nails down a chalkboard.

Aidan clapped his hands to his ears. "Yowza! What on earth?"

The sound erupted again. "I'm beginning to really miss the quiet London life," said Cagney. "I thought it was supposed to be *peaceful* in the country."

"It's the microphone," explained Lissy. "For tomorrow's fête."

"Is a fête like a fair?" asked Tess.

"I think so," said Lissy. "Weird word though, 'fête'."

"I like it," said Tess. "It rhymes with Nate and Kate and ...."

Cagney placed a hand over Tess' mouth.

Tess squeaked out one more word. "Late."

Lissy smiled. "I was going to say that you'd think it would mean destiny, but not in this case."

Tess poked her head around her cousin. The village green was now dotted with several stalls and a colorful marquee was being wrestled into place. At the far end sat a stage on which the offending microphone was being tested by an extremely disgruntled Major Puffin.

"The quick brown fox ..." bellowed the major, before the microphone squealed in pain.

The five bounded through the door of the Googly Gherkin. After the brightness of the day, the pub seemed exceptionally dark.

Aidan stayed still, waiting for his eyes to adjust. With its low ceilings and uneven floors, he wondered just how old the Googly Gherkin really was.

Cagney approached the empty bar. She was about to ding the bell, when Olivia caught her wrist. Cocking her head to the side, Olivia indicated a corridor from which voices could be heard - voices that sounded like they'd seen sunnier days.

"Good grief," said Cagney. "Everyone seems to be in a bad mood today."

Lissy sighed. *Maybe Cagney was right about the inbreeding thing.*

Sally's muffled voice floated along the corridor.

"You did what?" Nick roared.

"I told you. I rented out the guest rooms."

"What dya 'ave to go and do a thing like that for?"

"Oh! 'scuse me. I thought you'd be happy. All that work you've been doing up there, I thought you'd be glad of the extra cash."

"I can't believe it," Nick yelled.

"What was I meant to do? Tell the Featherington-Twits to stay at the Pickled Herring?"

"Now you're thinking."

"You've lost your 'ead, Nick Ratcliffe. You've gone bleedin' barmy. The F-Ts are opening the village fête tomorrow. Think they want to stay in Limpley-under-Water when the fair's on the village green, not ten feet away from where you're standing?"

"I don't care what the F-Ts want; they are *not* staying in my pub!"

"Oh! It's *your* pub now, is it? I'll have you know, my parents have lived in this village all their lives."

Cagney tapped Aidan on the shoulder. She mouthed the words *told you.*

"You arrive from the depths of London and think you bleedin' well own the place. Well, let me tell you this, Nick Ratcliffe. The Featherington-Twits are staying in this pub whether *you* like it or not." Sally flounced into the bar. Her face, scarlet and tight, matched her blouse perfectly.

Lissy tried a smile. "We were wondering, you know, if our bags …."

Sally looked up. Her eyes narrowed. Her lips formed a thin red line. "Not you lot again!"

Lissy took a step back.

"I thought Nick told you not to come sniffing around here. Do you never give up?"

Lissy gulped.

"Can't you leave us alone?" Sally banged her fist on the bar, exploding a bag of Hula Hoops.

"I … I …" Lissy stammered.

"I'm sorry, ma'am, just doing our job."

Lissy spun around. Filling the doorway was Inspector Watts and P.C. Pickle.

*
* *

29

Chase!

Nick came thundering down the hallway. "What d'ya want now?"

Aidan grabbed Lissy and dragged her out the way. Nick had been in a bad mood before. Aidan suspected the arrival of two policemen was not going to help improve it.

P.C. Pickle took a step forward and, before Tess could say prickly pear cactus jelly, reached behind his back and produced a pair of handcuffs. Nick took one glimpse at the dangling bracelets and bolted for the door, scattering both cousins and Sally as he went.

"Ow, me new shoes!" wailed Sally, as Nick landed heavily on a toe.

Nick did not seem to care much about Sally's new shoes. Nor did he care as his girlfriend tottered backwards into the arms of P.C. Pickle.

Nick gave the pair of them an almighty shove, and Sally and the constable went down like a pile of penguins. Sidestepping the squirming couple, Nick made a break for the door.

"After him!" shouted Inspector Watts, dashing towards the exit.

Tess peered at the tangled mass of bodies. P.C. Pickle lay flat on his back with Sally, floundering on top.

Tess tapped P.C. Pickle on the shoulder. "I might be wrong, but I think your boss wants you to chase him."

"Er ... yes ... right, oh. If I could maybe ... just possibly."

"Of course!" Sally tried to stand, but her left earring had become entwined in P.C. Pickle's hair. "If I could just get me ..."

"Absolutely ..."

"Oh for goodness sake!" Cagney disentangled Sally's earring and hoisted her onto her heels.

P.C. Pickle clambered to his feet. "He went that way," said Lissy, pointing towards the door.

"Most kind." Pickle adjusted his hat and sprinted out the door.

"He's over there!" Olivia jabbed a finger towards the village green. Nick was tearing across the grass towards a stall piled high with coconuts.

P.C. Pickle held onto his hat and started in pursuit. For someone so spindly he was an excellent runner and quickly overtook the older officer.

With P.C. Pickle barreling towards him, Nick made a beeline for the coconuts. Ducking behind the stall, he grabbed a coconut and tossed it directly at the constable, whacking him bang smack between the eyes. There was a dull thud as the coconut bounced off P.C. Pickle's head.

"Oooh, that's got to hurt," said Lissy, flinching.

"And hitting the ground is probably going to make it worse," said Tess, as the constable plummeted, nose-first into the grass.

Olivia watched as Nick abandoned the coconuts and made a dash towards the stage.

Another squeak emerged from the microphone. "She sells seashells, by the seashore," roared Major Puffin. He gave a sniff of satisfaction. "Yes. I think that'll do nicely."

Cagney swung around to face her cousins. "That Puffin really is the most oblivious man, isn't he? I mean, there's a police chase going on under his very nose and he's more concerned about checking the microphone."

"Yep," said Olivia. "Can't imagine him as a beef burger."

"Beefeater," corrected Lissy.

"I quite like him," said Tess. "Anyone who likes dogs is okay by me, right Olivia?"

Major Puffin replaced the microphone, strode across the stage and down the wooden steps. Scooping up three leashes, he waved to the cousins, his stick slicing through the air in salute.

By this point Nick was coming around the corner at full speed and didn't see the major as he bent to untangle a leash. Lissy closed her eyes and buried her face in Aidan's shirt.

Aidan started to call out, but it was too late as the two collided. In a move worthy of a circus performer, Nick cartwheeled over the major's back, before landing face first in the dirt. Major Puffin dropped the leashes and steadied himself. "What the blazes!"

Lissy opened an eye. "Is he okay?"

Olivia sprinted towards the stage and appraised the situation by giving Nick's head a gentle kick with her sneaker. "Nah! Just knocked out."

"I didn't see him coming," said Major Puffin, bewildered. "The man should be more careful. Can't go running around the countryside bumping into all and sundry, you know."

Nick raised his head. A bump the size of a peach was forming above his left eye. "You old fool! Why don't you look where yer going?"

Major Puffin's jaw dropped. You could see he was trying to say something, but nothing came out.

A dazed P.C. Pickle trotted up, clinked the handcuffs on Nick's wrists and hoisted him to his feet.

Squirming, Nick turned and directed his last words towards the speechless Puffin. "You're the one who should be locked up! What? Cat got your tongue? Bit too late for that now, isn't it? You blithering blabbermouth!"

"What's a blabbermouth?" asked Tess.

Before Aidan thought of an appropriate response, there was a whoop of pain. Turning, the cousins watched Buckingham sink his teeth into Nick's ankle. Nick tried to kick him off, but the corgi clung like a rat terrier, hanging on for dear life.

"Someone help!" cried Lissy, tearing towards the stage.

But she wasn't referring to either Buckingham or Nick. She was referring to Major Puffin, who had sunk to the ground, his hands shielding watery blue eyes.

30

The Search

L issy closed Spider and placed her on the bedside table. "I do hope Major P.'s going to be okay."

The cousins had traipsed across the green and an unhappy Sally had shown them where they would be sleeping. Two low-ceilinged bedrooms for the girls, one slightly larger room with an en suite for the Featherington-Twits and something Sally called a box room for Aidan.

"Course the major's going to be fine," said Cagney. "Well, you know, apart from being completely crazy. But there's not much you can do about that."

Buckingham had finally been persuaded to let go of Nick's leg and P.C. Pickle had marched the scowling man across the village green and hauled him off to jail.

"He should probably get a rabies shot," suggested Olivia.

"You think Buckingham has rabies?" mumbled Tess, her mouth stuffed with sausage roll.

Olivia grinned. "No, but Nick might. If I was Major P., I'd be dragging Buckingham to the vet for a complete course of antibiotics. When you've had your teeth into something as nasty as Nick, you can't be too careful."

Lissy shook her head. "I'm just worried about Major Puffin He didn't look good when they finally pried Nick's leg out of Buckingham's jaws."

"Nor would you if someone had just threatened to …." Olivia paused. "How did he phrase it?"

Lissy sighed. "Run his dogs through a mincer and grind his bones to dust."

Olivia grinned. "Oh yeah, that was it."

"No, that wasn't it," said Lissy. "It was something else. I mean, the man practically cried."

"Wuss!" said Cagney.

"But don't you think it's weird? Adults don't normally break down and cry because their dog bit someone," said Lissy.

"Oh, I don't know," said Cagney. "Aidan cries at the drop of a cat. Last week I misplaced his library book and he cried like a six-year-old."

"Hey!" said Tess. "I resemble that remark."

"I did *not* cry," said Aidan, indignantly. "I had allergies and, besides, you misplaced it in the swimming pool."

"I think it was something Nick said," suggested Lissy.

"I still don't think a grown man would cry over being called a blithering blabbermouth," said Cagney.

"Ah, forget about all that," said Olivia. "I'm more interested in the vegetable man, Dick Turnip."

"Turpin," corrected Lissy.

Aidan closed his book on English slang. "Yep, I wonder why Nick insisted he hadn't stayed here. Seems rather odd."

Cagney plopped herself onto the overstuffed chair. "What? Some old guy from, like, the twelfth…"

"Seventeenth," said Lissy.

"Like I said. Some old guy in the seventeenth century robs the rich and gives to the poor. What's odd about that?"

"That's Robin," said Aidan.

"That's what I said. Robs from the rich and gives to the poor."

"He means Robin Hood," said Lissy.

Cagney waved a dismissive hand. "Details."

"You'd think Nick would know. I mean he *does* live here," said Aidan. "At least, he used to."

"Maybe he was mistaken?" said Olivia. "People make mistakes all the time. Like when I confused Austria with Australia in that Geography exam. It could happen to anyone."

"Kangaroos do *not* live in Salzburg," said Lissy.

"They don't know that for sure," said Olivia. "Personally, I think they've just not looked hard enough."

"Tess could you possibly eat more food?" asked Lissy.

Tess was nestled between the bedcovers, surrounded by half-eaten pieces of pastry.

"They're just so good. The pastry's so flaky and the meat is so meaty and ..."

"Why don't we save some of these for later?" said Lissy, scooping up the remains and placing them on the dresser. "Honestly, Tess, there's enough food here to feed a small country! Or even a relatively large one."

"Sure," said Tess. "I just want to look for the secret room. The one Lissy read about in the library."

"I'd forgotten about that," said Olivia, flicking crumbs off her pillow. "What are we waiting for? Let's find it."

"It can't be that easy," said Lissy. "I'm sure people have searched."

Olivia smiled. "Yeah, but *we* have experience."

Lissy examined her watch; it was still early. "I guess we've got nothing else to do."

"Okay, let's split up," said Cagney. "Lissy will search our room. Olivia and Tess will search this room. And Aidan can search that teeny, tiny, ridiculously small, couldn't swing a mouse in it room in the shape of a box."

"What are we looking for?" asked Olivia.

"Access to a secret room," said Cagney. "How hard can it be?"

Aidan shook his head. "Seeing you've assigned rooms to everyone else, I assume that means you're going to search Sally's and the Featherington-Twits' rooms?"

Cagney dropped to her knees, lifted a flowery dust ruffle and stuck her head under the bed. "Erm, no! I'll help here."

The cousins had searched rooms before and were getting good at it. First they checked the floor, then the walls, finally the ceiling. Nooks, crannies and even mouse holes were pushed, prodded and generally interrogated. Twenty minutes later the five were back in Olivia and Tess' room looking slightly worse for wear. Aidan was covered in cobwebs and Cagney nursed a severely bruised toe.

"Don't ask," murmured Cagney, hobbling across the uneven floors. "I had a fight with that huge ugly closet."

"Let me guess," said Aidan. "The huge ugly closet won?"

Tess sprung across the room and leapt onto the bed. "To be specific, it whooped her! I'm surprised it didn't land on her."

"Actually, the English call that a wardrobe," said Lissy, admiring the mahogany armoire that dominated the room.

"Well, it certainly went to war with me," said Cagney, limping towards the chair.

"Did you find anything?" Olivia asked Aidan.

Aidan grabbed a towel and started to swipe away months of spider activity. He groaned. Aidan hated dirt. Especially when it clung to him. "Diddly squat!"

Tess giggled. "Diddly what?"

"It's English for absolutely nothing," said Aidan, grinning.

Lissy glanced at Aidan. "You're getting an English accent."

"Indubitably," said Aidan.

"Watch it, or soon you'll be sounding like a Twit," said Cagney.

Olivia grinned. "Which one?"

"Makes no difference," said Lissy. "They sound exactly the same."

Olivia suddenly remembered there'd been something she'd been meaning to ask Aidan. *Something about English words, but what was it?*

Cagney started to pace the room. "Then the entrance must be hidden in either Sally's or the Featherington-Twits' room. Who's going to volunteer to take a look?"

Aidan's head disappeared behind his book of Cockney rhyming slang. Tess studied her pink welly boots, and Lissy suddenly found something incredibly interesting on Spider. It seemed nobody wanted to search the Twits' room - or worse, be found snooping in Sally's.

Olivia shrugged. "I guess we'll have to draw straws."

31

Caught!

"urry up!" whispered Cagney.

"I am hurrying. Of course, I might be hurrying a bit faster if someone came in and helped me."

Cagney opened the door a fraction wider. "Someone's got to be on lookout."

"Yes, someone! But all four of you?"

The cousins had drawn straws. Lissy had drawn the straw for Sally's room and had methodically searched it with no outcome. Aidan had drawn the straw for the last room: the Twits.

Aidan's head bobbed up from behind an ornate floral footrest. A brown blob stained the end of his nose. A cobweb hung from his ear.

Cagney stifled a smile. "You can never be too vigilant. Just keep searching. Remember, we have a system. Lissy's in the bar with Spider. If the F-Ts come in she's going to whistle the Star Spangled Banner to Olivia, who is situated at the bottom of the stairs. Olivia will wave to Tess at the top of the stairs, who will nod her head in my direction, indicating a Twit has entered the building."

"Not nod." Tess skipped along the corridor. "We said shake."

Cagney rolled her eyes. "We definitely said nod."

"Well, I'm not nodding." Tess sidestepped Cagney and peeked through the door. "I don't want to look like one of those toys Mrs. Snoops has in the back of her car."

"Nod, shake, does it really matter?" said Cagney, her temper rising.

"How about I do this?" Tess pirouetted so high she almost lost a welly.

Cagney exhaled. Turning to face Tess, she leapt into the air, flapped her arms and waggled her head all in one spectacular motion. "I don't care if you jump down, turn around and fly to El Paso as long as I can see you."

"Is that some kind of newfangled American dance?" asked the voice behind her. "It's extremely athletic."

Cagney spun around, readjusted her glasses and stared into the twinkling eyes of Lord Featherington-Twit.

"Erm! Yep! It's a type of two-step. Very popular in Texas," stammered Cagney, glancing behind her. Tess was nowhere to be seen.

Lord Featherington-Twit reached for the handle.

Cagney threw herself in his path. "You should definitely not go in there."

Featherington-Twit paused. "Excuse me?"

"What I mean is," Cagney sniffed the air, "do you smell gas?"

"No!"

"Skunks?"

"My dear young lady, I am happy to report I smell none of the above, especially as skunks do not reside in England."

"Oh yeah! Darn, I forgot that bit."

"Now, if you don't mind, I would very much like to grab forty winks before Henri finds me and drags me off to inspect something else for the blasted fête."

"Absolutely!" Cagney stuck her head around the door and scanned the room. One four-poster bed, one ornate closet; wait, make that wardrobe. One overstuffed chair and not a single cousin. *Where, in the name of Great Aunt Maud, were they?*

Cagney took a step to the side. "Yep, fit for a King. Well, a lord. I'll just ... er .... close your curtains for you." Cagney strode towards the lead-studded windows. Grabbing the silk drapes, Cagney dragged them together. "There you go. All settled."

Featherington-Twit crossed to the bed and tested the springs lightly with his hands. "Most obliged."

"Night then. Sleep well. Don't let the bedbugs fight," said Cagney with one of her typical misquotes. Crossing the room, Cagney said a silent prayer that Lord Featherington-Twit would fall asleep quickly and, if possible, not notice the pink wellies and brown loafers jutting out below his curtains.

*
*
*

32

Trapped

Cagney edged backwards out of the room and felt a hand on her shoulder.

"What have you done with Aidan and Tess?" asked Lissy, spinning her cousin round.

Cagney looked sheepish as her thumb indicated the Featherington-Twits' room.

Lissy's eyes widened.

"Behind the curtains."

"Not exactly original," said Olivia, jogging down the corridor.

Lissy was distraught. "You *left* them in there?"

"What else was I supposed to do? I could hardly smuggle them out."

"Don't worry," said Olivia. "Henri said Basil falls asleep at the drop of a coronet. Whatever that is."

Lissy gasped. "What were they thinking?"

"Do you really think I have any idea what my brother is thinking? Ever? And don't even get me started on Tess."

"You have a point," said Lissy.

There was a rumble from behind the door.

Lissy looked alarmed. "Please tell me that's not Tess' stomach?"

Olivia put her ear to the door. She had an encyclopedic knowledge of the sounds of Tess' internal plumbing. "Nope, not Tess."

"It's Basil," said Cagney. "He's snoring."

Lissy blew out a sigh. "Oh, thank goodness."

Olivia scanned her watch. "Then I'll give them five, four, three, two—"

The door inched open and Aidan and Tess slid through the gap.

Cagney turned to face Tess. "What were you thinking?"

"I panicked."

"But what happened?" asked Lissy. "How did Lord Featherington-Twit get this far without Aidan getting out. What happened to our plan?"

"I'll tell you what happened." Cagney pointed at Tess. "Someone left their post."

"It wasn't my fault," said Tess.

"Then whose fault was it?" asked Olivia.

Tess wrinkled her nose. "Okay, so technically it might have been my fault, but I'm six. What do you expect?"

Cagney removed her glasses and gave them a quick polish. She turned to Aidan. "Did you find anything?"

Aidan swiped a smudge of dirt off his nose. "Not a thing."

The five ambled along the corridor. As they turned the corner, a figure emerged from the gloom.

Olivia stepped forward. "Hey, what are *you* doing here?"

The person paused. Slowly, they turned. "Well hello, you," said Rupert, stepping from the shadows.

"Are you looking for *us*?" asked Aidan.

Rupert seemed confused. "Yes! No! I mean ... I was searching for Sally."

Lissy frowned. "She's in the bar."

"Is she? Must have missed her. What are *you* guys doing here?"

"We're staying here," said Aidan.

"Castle Featherington-Twit not good enough anymore?" said Rupert, nudging Aidan playfully.

"Not 'til the plumbing gets fixed," said Olivia. "Although showering in my opinion is highly overrated."

"Not in mine it's not," said Cagney.

Tess sniffed the air. "Does anybody smell anything?"

Rupert glanced behind him.

Tess edged forward and sniffed again. "I can smell a ham sandwich."

"Nobody can smell a ham sandwich," said Rupert, laughing.

"Tess can," said Aidan.

Tess peeked behind Rupert's back.

"Oh!" said Rupert, pulling an Upper Crust bag from behind his back. "*This* ham sandwich."

"Told ya," said Tess, proudly.

"I was going for a, erm, picnic. Thought I'd stop by and see if Sally, you know, wanted to come with me."

"A picnic with one ham sandwich?" said Tess, her eyes widening. "I need to show you how to picnic *Texas* style."

"I don't think Sally's in the mood," said Aidan.

"Pickle arrested Nick," said Tess, eyeing the familiar brown bag.

Lissy frowned. "Besides, she has to work in the bar."

"Course she does! Stupid idea. Maybe another time." And with that, Rupert Smythe turned and fled down the hall.

"What's got into him?" asked Aidan.

"I have absolutely no idea," said Lissy.

"I think he has a crush on Sally," said Tess. "Rupert and Sally sitting in a tree, K I S S …"

"Nick's not going to like *that* very much," said Olivia, dragging her still-singing sister into their room.

"That's the understatement of the century. Did you see the look Nick gave Rupert yesterday?" said Lissy.

"Poor Rupert," said Cagney. "He's so nice."

Lissy rolled her eyes. "You mean he's so cute."

Cagney gazed dreamily at her cousin. "Yeah, that too."

Aidan slumped into the armchair. "Does anyone feel like we're missing something?"

Lissy shrugged. "Yep, but don't ask me what."

"It might be nothing," said Olivia. "But do you remember when we first went into Odds and Ends? I could have sworn on the name of Great Aunt Maud that there was someone behind the curtain with Rupert. I could hear them talking."

"Maybe he was chatting to a friend," suggested Lissy.

"Then why would he lock a friend in the store when he left to play cricket?"

"The shop has two stories. Maybe Rupert lives above it and his friend stayed there," said Aidan.

"Maybe," said Olivia, frowning. "But then the other night, when I went to the church, I heard the same voice again and Rupert was also there."

"You didn't tell me," said Aidan.

"I didn't think it was important, but now I'm not so sure."

"You're crazy," said Cagney. "It's just Rupert."

Olivia shook her head. "I may not be as good at accents as Aidan, but I'm telling you, there was someone other than Rupert behind the curtain and I want to know who."

*
* *

33

Break-In

Sally plunked an extra large portion of bangers and mash in front of Tess. "Are you sure she can eat all that? Are you sure she's not going to explode?"

"Trust us," said Olivia. "The girl could eat for England."

"On your head be it!" Sally turned to Henri and motioned towards her plate. "Oh, and sorry about the substitution, but for some reason all the pickles have gone missing."

"Your health," said Lord Featherington-Twit raising his pint. Henri and the cousins clinked glasses and tucked in. Tess was not the only one with food. The entire table buckled beneath the best the Googly Gherkin could offer.

All through dinner Basil kept the cousins entertained with stories of his childhood in Bumble Bottom, embellished by Henri's wild tales of village life.

Olivia snorted lemonade up her nose as Lord Featherington-Twit recounted stories of the rivalry between the owner of The Upper Crust and the Mouse House. And Aidan almost fell off his chair when Henri recalled the story of Penelope Snodgrass and the indignant duck. Even Cagney was laughing by the time dessert came.

Aidan nudged Olivia and pointed towards the bar. "Look, there's Rupert."

Henri lifted her spoon and tucked into the most delicious smelling apple pie. "He really is the most handsome man, isn't he? I have to tell you, the ladies of Bumble Bottom were not displeased when Mr. Smythe leased the antique store two years ago, remember Basil?"

"Yes, yes my dear," said Basil, who was still delighting Tess with his impression of a disgruntled duck.

"Sally said he tried to buy half the furniture in the pub. Don't blame him. It's probably worth a small fortune," said Henri.

"What, those rickety old beds and that horrible old closet?" asked Cagney, remembering her bruised toe.

Henri brushed a splattering of whipped cream from Tess' cheek. "Some of that furniture is as old as the Googly Gherkin itself. And that's saying something."

Soon the meal was finished and conversation exhausted.

Basil put down his cup. "Bedtime, I think, my dear."

Henri rose. "Don't stay up too late, now. Remember we have the fête tomorrow." Henri beamed at Tess. "Plus, I may have a small surprise for you."

Basil and Henri waved goodnight to Sally, who was leaning over the bar handing Rupert a menu.

"She doesn't look like she's missing Nick too much, does she?" said Aidan.

Tess glanced up from blowing bubbles in her soda. "Nope!"

Rupert's hearty laugh floated towards them.

"In fact," said Olivia, "it looks like Rupert's going to be here for a while. Which gives me time to do a little snooping."

Lissy shook her head. "I'm having nothing to do with any snooping."

"Nor me," said Cagney, who had not taken her eyes off the handsome man since he walked in.

Olivia turned to Aidan.

"Nuh huh. No way. Absolutely not!"

"Hold it still," said Olivia.

"I *am* holding it still," said Aidan.

"Then hold it stiller."

Aidan shifted the ladder before glaring up at his cousin. "Dang it, Olivia, I think I got a splinter."

"Sssh, I'm almost in."

"For goodness sake hurry, before you wake the entire neighborhood."

"Got it," said Olivia, raising the latch and toppling through the window.

Aidan sighed. How he'd got talked into this he'd never know. But Olivia could be persuasive and, before he knew it, Aidan was being dragged down the High Street and along the alleyway backing onto Odds and Ends.

The village was deserted. Potts, lurking in the hedgerow, being the only sign of life. Both cousins had said hello, but Potts was not in a 'hello' type of mood and promptly turned his back.

For someone who'd just been robbed, Mr. Smythe didn't seem particularly concerned with safety. It had taken Olivia a mere second to find the unlocked gate leading to a non-descript backyard. Not a single light illuminated the property; not a single puppy dog guarded it.

First Olivia had peeked in the downstairs window. Then she had tried the back door. Finally she'd spotted a rickety ladder and, with Aidan's help, walked it towards the building, right underneath a second-story window that had been left alluringly ajar.

"This is *not* a good idea," said Aidan, examining the tiny splinter in his thumb. "You do remember the police arrested someone for doing the exact same thing? Someone who landed in jail."

"Sssh!" said Olivia, reappearing at the window. "I'm not stealing anything. I just took a quick peek."

Olivia shoved her legs out the window and wiggled backwards. Finding the uppermost rung, she shifted her weight onto the ladder. There was an almighty crack and Olivia started to flail.

Aidan looked upwards and immediately wished he hadn't.

"Watch out for the—" Olivia didn't get to finish, as the wooden rung hit Aidan squarely on the head.

"What are you doing?" asked Aidan, rubbing his forehead and muttering words Olivia had never heard him use before.

Olivia's legs seemed to be doing some kind of shimmy. "What do you *think* I'm doing?" came the muffled reply.

"Right now I think you're trying to kill yourself. But I've been wrong before."

The legs wiggled some more. "I'll just see if I can get back ... uh oh."

Aidan shut his eyes. "Do not 'uh oh' me, Olivia Puddleton. Get down from there immediately."

Olivia was silent. Her body wriggled. Her legs flapped, but she neither came out of the window nor went back in.

"You're stuck, aren't you?"

"Might be."

"Of all the hair-brained, stupid ..."

"Ssssh!" said Olivia.

"Don't you sssh me!"

"SSSSHHH!"

Aidan frowned. "Why?"

Aidan barely spoke the question before the downstairs lights flickered on, illuminating him like the Rockefeller Christmas tree.

Olivia grimaced. "That's why!"

34

Figuring it Out

Olivia stood in the bedroom doorway. Her shorts were ripped, her tee covered in something wet. Her hair was, even for her, a disaster.

Cagney backed away from her cousin. "Is that blood?"

Olivia swiped a finger across her cheek. "Yep. But I don't think it's mine." Olivia strode towards the bed and flopped backwards.

Cagney poked her head into the corridor and regarded the deserted hallway. "What have you done with my brother?"

"Oh, he'll be here soon. He's having a bit of trouble getting up the stairs."

Lissy spun to face her disheveled cousin. "What do you mean? He can't get up the stairs? What have you done to him?"

The door swung open and Aidan leaned against the threshold, tottering ever so slightly to the left. Blood trickled down his forehead.

"See, I told you he'd be along in a minute."

Lissy gasped. "What did she do to you?"

Droplets of blood plopped onto the wood floor. Aidan's right eye started to swell and the entire left side of his face was beginning to turn purple. Without saying a word, Aidan lurched forward and crumpled to the floor.

"You could have been killed," said Lissy, who had helped pull Aidan onto a chair.

Cagney choked. "I'm never that lucky."

Lissy scowled. "You should've let Olivia get down by herself. Nothing bad *ever* happens to her. You should know that by now. I think they did something to her in China. Some kind of disaster-resistant superpower."

"She's indestructible," said Tess. "Or at least, that's what Dad says."

"So how *did* you get down?" asked Lissy.

Olivia grinned. "Aidan managed to climb the few remaining rungs and pull me out the window."

Aidan shook his head. "Unfortunately, that's when the ladder decided to die."

"Yep," said Olivia. "Poor ladder."

A sound best described as a growl escaped Aidan's lips.

"You're a lot softer than you look," said Olivia.

Aidan scowled. "You're a lot heavier than *you* look."

Olivia grinned. "It's just a few scratches. Besides, it was worth it. I found out what I needed to know."

Cagney rolled her eyes. "And what was that?"

"Who Rupert was talking to in the store. And why I couldn't see them in the graveyard."

"Why?" said Lissy. "Who is it?"

Olivia gazed around the room. "It's nobody."

There was silence. Tess gave the end of her nose a good rub, looking around expectantly.

Cagney finally broke the silence. "Nobody? What do you mean, nobody? It's got to be *somebody*, or are they a ghost too?"

"Kinda," said Olivia.

"But Rupert has to be talking to *someone.* You've heard them, you've practically seen them," said Aidan.

"But I haven't, have I? I've never seen them. They mysteriously disappear, and the reason why they disappear? Well, it's obvious, isn't it? They don't exist."

The others stared at Olivia with not even the daybreak of comprehension, not alone the dawn.

"It's Rupert I've been hearing. The voice that sounds like Billy. It's Rupert's."

"That's crazy" said Cagney. "You're out of your mind."

"But why would he try to sound like Billy?" asked Lissy.

"Doesn't make any sense," said Aidan.

"I know. But it's the only answer. I went to Odds and Ends tonight to see if there was somewhere Rupert would leave a friend when he went to play cricket. But there wasn't. Just boxes and boxes of antiques piled all higgledy piggledy."

"I love that word," said Tess, munching a sticky bun.

"At both Odds and Ends *and* in the graveyard it was just Rupert. There *was* no one else. I couldn't put it together until tonight. But when I got stuck in the window, I heard the same voice again. Then, when we were leaving, I looked back. I could see Rupert, but there was no one with him. No one, but his phone."

"Of course," said Lissy, comprehension registering in her eyes.

"So he's putting on a voice and trying to sound like someone else?" said Aidan. "But why is he pretending to be someone he's not?"

"And who's he talking to on the phone?" said Cagney.

Olivia shrugged. "That you're going to have to figure out for yourselves."

35

Ghosts

Tess poked her sister. "Are you awake?"

"No!"

"Are you sure?"

Olivia rolled over and came face to feet with her sister. "What do you want?"

Tess hoisted herself into a sitting position. "I want to know if you believe in ghosts?"

"Of course I don't," Olivia paused. "Well, I never used to."

It was their first night in the Googly Gherkin. After the revelation of the night before the subject had turned to ghosts and, in the stillness of the night, Tess began to wish it hadn't.

"Do you think they're friendly?"

Olivia removed a flake of pastry from between her toes. "How should I know?"

"I bet they are. Just because they're trapped between worlds, unable to find peace, doesn't mean they have to be mean."

"Actually, if I was trapped somewhere between life and death I think I would be very mean."

Tess nodded. Olivia wasn't in the same league as Cagney, but she definitely had a cranky streak.

"Why are people scared of ghosts?"

Olivia shrugged. "I guess they're scared of the unknown?"

"It seems kind of silly."

"Well, they also might be scared of all the moaning and wailing and rattling of chains," said Olivia.

"But why do you think ghosts only come out at night? Do you think it's because they sleep during the day?"

"I don't think ghosts sleep," said Olivia, plumping her pillow.

"So you don't think ghosts can hurt you? You don't think they lie awake all day plotting to scare you at night?"

Olivia thought about it. "Well, I didn't up to now."

Aidan pulled the eiderdown up to his nose and wished the Googly Gherkin wasn't quite so old. He never worried about ghosts in his 1980s ranch house. For one thing, the A/C blocked out anything that might be considered a ghostly draft. So why was it here, in a coaching inn dating back to the fifteenth century, he felt so afraid?

Lissy was sure there was some kind of animal scratching in the rafters. *Probably a squirrel, but a very large squirrel. What about those skunky badger things? Could they climb?* Lissy doubted it, but made a mental note to research it on Spider tomorrow.

Cagney lay flat on her back, her eyes darting around the room. With the pub drained of people, the creaks and squeaks sounded oh so loud. A shadow passed across the window and she felt her heart quicken. *Was that the silhouette of a woman? A woman in white?*

There was a loud clunk above Cagney's head. She searched her brain. *What had Sally said about noises?* The clunk clunked again. Cagney pulled a pillow over her head and decided, ghost or no ghost, it was time to get some sleep.

By the time the door opened there was no one awake to witness it. Into the passageway drifted a ghostly specter. The apparition floated along the corridor, turned the corner and disappeared.

*

Tess awoke with a start. All this talk of ghosts left her hungry. Tess wrinkled her nose and gave an almighty sniff. Somewhere in this room lay the remains of a jelly donut. Tess wrestled with the idea of getting out of bed, but it was cold and her pink fuzzy slippers were nowhere in sight. Her tummy let out a grumble. It was no good. She would have to find food.

Ah, now she remembered. Lissy had placed the remainders of a sticky bun and a half-eaten sausage roll on the dresser. Sitting up, Tess realized someone had beaten her to it, because slumped in the puffy arm chair, dressed in a feathered cap and velvet jacket, sat Dick Turpin, half a sticky bun poking from his lips.

36

The Fête

Tess dropped her spoon into the empty cereal bowl. "But I'm telling you, I saw Dick Turnip."

"Turpin," corrected Lissy.

"Him too," said Tess.

"And I saw King Henry the Eighth," said Cagney.

"You did?" asked Tess.

Cagney gave her a look.

Tess folded her arms across her pink stripy dress and looked defiant. "He ate the rest of my sausage roll and I have the crumbs to prove it."

"Right," said Cagney, "I saw what you did to that sausage roll. There's no way anyone – not even a ghost would finish *that* off."

"Did too," said Tess, "then he disappeared into the wall."

Olivia rolled her eyes. "He's either a real person eating or a ghost disappearing. He can't be both."

Lissy placed an arm around Tess' shoulder. "It was a long day. Maybe you were dreaming, especially after our chat last night. To be honest, I spent the night thinking I could hear something above me."

"And I thought I heard someone walking along the corridor," said Aidan.

Lissy smiled at her youngest cousin. "I'd just forget it if I were you, Tess."

The cousins were sitting on the picnic benches watching the activity on the village green. Overnight, tents and stalls had been erected and, with thousands of miniature Union Jacks fluttering in the breeze, they gave the entire village a superbly festive feel.

Cagney slammed down her teacup. "Okay, so our plan is to follow Rupert and see what he's up to."

Aidan nodded. "We'll divide into pairs. Two can follow and two can stay here in case he goes upstairs again."

Tess held up her fingers as she figured out the division. "But two into five doesn't go. There's one left over. Who's going to be the leftover?"

Cagney scowled. "Who do you think?"

"That's okay," said Tess. "I've decided blending in is not my strong point."

Olivia surveyed her sister, who today wore pink and white polka-dot leggings under her pink stripy dress and the glitziest pair of cowboy boots to have ever escaped from Texas. Her shiny black hair hung free, and perched atop it teetered a voluminous bow.

"I'll just go to the fête," said Tess. "Henri says they have palm reading, a coconut shy *and* a tombola."

"A what?" asked Olivia.

"A coconut shy is where you throw balls at a coconut and try to make it fall off its perch," explained Lissy.

"Like what Nick threw at P.C Pickle?" asked Tess.

"Exactly like that," said Lissy.

"And a tombola?" asked Tess.

Lissy shrugged. "Absolutely no idea."

Cagney threw her camera strap over her shoulder. "All right, Lissy and I will take the first shift, then we'll trade at noon. I'm assuming he's not going anywhere too far, with the stupid carnival and everything."

"There he is." Aidan pulled his baseball cap low as Rupert, dressed in a pair of jeans and an extremely confident jacket, appeared from behind the hedge.

"Go on then," said Olivia. "Get going."

As Rupert rounded the corner, Lissy and Cagney casually rose.

Rupert waved to the cousins, before heading across the green towards the church.

Cagney and Lissy slipped from behind the picnic table and started to follow, as Rupert quickened his pace through the stalls.

"Oh look, there's Potts," said Tess, waving with enthusiasm.

The tramp emerged from behind the hedge. Improbably, his clothes looked dirtier, his hair, wilder, and his face, filthier. Potts scowled at the cousins, before heading in the same direction as Cagney and Lissy. Close on his heels came a jingling sound.

"I recognize that jingle," said Tess, as several men decorated in bells appeared from behind the hedge.

"It's like a parade," said Aidan, as the Morris Men jingled their way onto the village green.

"This place has been a complete ghost town, sorry, ghost village," said Aidan. "Who knew a little fair would be so popular?"

In the past hour there had been a trickle of visitors, which had grown into a steady stream and now, as the clock ticked towards eleven, approached a torrent. Villagers, children and pirates littered most of the green, along with one rather confused-looking llama. An exuberant brass band suddenly eclipsed the gentle hum, and the owner of the Upper Crust threatened Major Puffin with bodily harm if he didn't back away from fiddling with the microphone.

At 10:55 the doors to the Googly Gherkin flew open and Lord and Lady Featherington-Twit strode down the steps.

"Oooh, you look pretty," said Tess, rising to greet them.

"Thank you," said Lord Featherington-Twit.

Henri pursed her lips. "She meant me, you big oaf!"

Basil gave Tess a wink.

Henri had on her best frock, a chiffon lilac affair teamed with a sturdy pair of shoes. Her long pale hair had been swept into an elegant chignon and partially covered by a billowing feathery hat.

"Never know what to wear," said Henri, squishing down a feather. "Anyway, can't stand around chit-chatting. Basil and I have a fête to open."

"That we do, my dear." Featherington-Twit offered Henri his arm and they headed towards the stage.

At that exact moment, Lissy and Cagney came careening around the corner.

"Did you see him?" Clutching her stomach and red in the face, Cagney stumbled towards the bench and flung herself down. As her head plopped onto the picnic table it was obvious that wherever they'd been, there'd been mud. Lots of mud.

"You lost him?" asked Olivia.

Cagney's head barely moved, but Aidan was pretty sure she was giving Olivia a look.

"It was like he knew we were behind him," said Lissy, picking some kind of vegetation from her curls. "We followed him to the church, the library, across a stream, around a field ..."

"A field with pigs," said Cagney.

"Yes, lots of pigs," continued Lissy.

"I think he took you on a wild duck chase," said Aidan.

"Goose," said Lissy.

"Bless you," said Cagney.

"Oh, there was a pond too." Lissy took off a sneaker and turned it over. Several pebbles and a startled snail clattered onto the cobblestones.

"But you lost him?" asked Aidan.

Cagney's head rose an inch off the picnic table. "Not exactly lost, more misplaced."

Lissy blew a curl off her forehead. "Yep, we misplaced him somewhere between the pig sty and the cowshed."

"What was the owner of an antique store doing in a cowshed?" asked Olivia.

"No idea, but he's not there anymore," said Tess.

"He's not?" asked Aidan.

Tess pointed towards the Googly Gherkin. "Not unless there are two of him."

Cagney's head jerked upwards. There, striding down the steps, his auburn hair gleaming in the sun, was Rupert Smythe.

37

Fancy Dress

O kay, we'll let the experts take it from here," said Olivia. "Come on, Aidan."

"Do I have to?" Aidan turned to Lissy and pointed to his face. "Look what happened to me last time."

Lissy made a mental note to research black eyes and see how long they lasted. Although, to be fair, Aidan's eye was less black and more a delicate purpley yellow.

"You'll be fine," said Cagney.

"Then you go with her," said Aidan.

Cagney didn't move.

"Olivia, promise you won't beat up Aidan," said Lissy.

"I didn't beat him up. I just fell on him. There's a significant difference."

Aidan muttered something about ladders and flailing legs, but to be honest he wasn't making too much sense.

"Are you coming or not?" said Olivia.

"If I have to." Aidan stepped over the seat of the picnic bench and sighed. "Once more into the breach, dear friends."

"I thought you said we were nowhere near the sea," said Olivia.

Aidan sighed.

"'Ere, where d'ya think you lot are going?"

Aidan turned towards the Googly Gherkin. "Excuse me?"

Sally stood, hands on hips. "Get ya sorry selves inside and put on those clothes Lady Henrietta left for you."

"Henri left us clothes?" asked Lissy.

"She sure did," said Sally, hiding a smile. "In fact, she went to a lot of trouble to make sure you'd be suitably dressed for the, er, occasion."

"Is she joking?" asked Olivia, whose idea of dressing up consisted of wearing two-day-old jeans and a semi-clean shirt.

"She doesn't look like she's joking," said Tess, "but, to be honest, it's hard to tell with these English."

The cousins filed back into the pub.

"You'll find them on the F-Ts' bed," said Sally, heading towards the bar. "And make sure you come down and show me, like, before you head to the carnival."

The five traipsed up the narrow wooden stairs and along the uneven corridor. They stood outside the Featherington-Twits' door.

"Should we knock?" asked Lissy.

Tess turned the handle. "We didn't last time."

The five entered the room and stared. Then they stared some more.

"Well, don't you all look splendid," said Sally, her eyes widening by the second.

Lissy, Aidan and Olivia stood in a row, expressionless. Tess was busy spinning, her wings flapping, her headpiece glistening.

"I can't believe Henri got us these costumes," squealed Tess. "This must be the surprise she mentioned yesterday."

"Go on then, give us a twirl," said Sally, trying to gain composure and failing.

"Tell her I don't twirl," Olivia whispered to Lissy.

"I don't know why you're complaining," said Aidan. "You're not the one wearing a dress."

"Yes, but you're not the one with a pink bow around their neck," hissed Olivia.

"I'm wearing a mask! With feathers!" continued Aidan.

"Ah, stop your whining," said Olivia. "At least it hides your black eye."

Lissy gave up trying to adjust her oversized nose and turned to examine Olivia's spots. "I thought you liked animals."

Olivia scowled. "I like fried chicken. Doesn't mean I want to dress like one."

"You all look marvelous," said Sally, "one of you's bound to win."

"Win what?" asked Tess, jigging up and down. "Are there prizes?"

"The fancy dress competition, of course. The F-Ts thought you might like to take part. You get to go up on stage and everything."

"The fancy what?" said Olivia, doing a one-eighty towards the stairs.

Aidan grabbed her tail. "I don't think so, lady. If I'm going out there in tights, you're going out in a tail."

"It's a competition to see who has the fanciest costume." Sally frowned. "Wait, weren't there five of you?"

"Yes, ma'am," said Lissy. "Cagney's having … well, she's having a few issues with her fanciness."

A muffled bump, followed by a yelp sounded from the stairs. Cagney emerged from the gloom. From what little you could see of her - she did not look happy.

"Beautiful," said Sally, smothering a smile. "Just lovely." Sally turned and fled behind the counter.

"Go on then, get a move on. Competition starts at 11:45 sharp."

"Well, I guess this explains the pirates," said Aidan, heading towards the door.

Cagney hung back.

"Come on," said Lissy, crossing her fingers, "it doesn't look that bad."

Cagney growled.

"Yeah." Tess ran a hand over Cagney's fuzzy stomach. "It brings out your softer side."

Cagney gave her the look of death.

"With that amount of padding, at least no one's going to recognize you," said Olivia, trying to keep still so her tail didn't wag.

Cagney stared at Aidan. "Do you have anything to add?"

Aidan shook his head. "I'm one bird's nest short of a tree. I have no judgment."

"Come on," said Tess, skipping across the lane. "It's going to be fun."

Cagney sighed. "I may be wrong, but I seriously doubt that.

38

Marla the Magnificent

The village green had now reached capacity. Stalls were open for trade and the Limpley-under-Water brass band was in full swing. Young girls skipped around a large pole, weaving a pattern with brightly colored ribbons and various children wandered through the stalls all dressed in a variety of weird and wonderful costumes.

Aidan uncovered his watch. "We have ten minutes before the competition. Let's see if we can find Rupert."

"I don't know how we're supposed to follow Rupert, guard the Googly Gherkin and be in a stupid competition all at the same time," said Cagney.

"Well, there's nothing we can do now. We can't let the F-Ts down; they've been so kind," said Lissy.

"We'll just have to do the best we can and keep an eye out for Rupert. Well, all except Cagney who has a slight visual impairment right now." Aidan grabbed his sister and steered her away from the shaggy dog competition. Some of the dogs were starting to snarl and one sniffed her footwear with significant interest.

"Let's get her away from the animals," said Lissy. "There's something about that color they just don't like."

"I think it's the smell," said Olivia. "She smells kind of funny."

"You know I can hear you, right?" said Cagney, as Aidan guided her across the grass.

"This area should be safe," said Lissy, heading towards various booths.

The cousins wandered in and out of the stands. There were stalls selling jam, booths selling cakes and tables piled high with masses of strawberries and cream. If you got far enough away from Cagney's costume the smell of baked goods was intoxicating. Lissy feared Tess would go into overload.

Farther along there were stalls displaying various groups of fruits and vegetables. Women with clipboards were judging the length, breadth and glossiness of something Lissy suspected was either a parsnip or a turnip. She really needed to go back to the Googly Gherkin and do some serious root vegetable research.

Cagney stopped abruptly. "What's that noise?"

Lissy stared at her feet. "I think it's my shoes. They have some kind of squeak."

"Can you unsqueak them?"

Lissy gave Cagney a look.

Cagney shrugged. "I'll take that as a no."

"We're not exactly incognito," said Olivia, disentangling a small child from her tail.

"This is crazy," said Cagney. "How on earth are we supposed to sneak up on anyone dressed like …. well, this?"

The cousins had reached the section of the fair with games. To their right were two enthusiastic pirates trying to knock coconuts off their perches.

To their left, sat a colorful bouncy castle and several squealing children. Tucked away in a corner sat a diaphanous-looking tent with an easel proclaiming *Marla the Magnificent, Fortune Teller to the Stars*.

Olivia gazed longingly towards the tractor rides. Aidan wouldn't have minded having a go at the tombola - whatever that was.

They passed another pirate, this one with an impressive wooden leg and a parrot which took one look at Cagney, and flew off.

"Wow, the people of Bumble Bottom really take this fancy dress competition seriously," said Lissy, fluffing her pompoms.

Tess grabbed hold of Olivia's tail and gave it a yank. "I want to get my fortune read."

"I don't think we have time," said Aidan, studying his watch.

"But I want to see if I'm going to grow up to be a fairy."

"If you don't pipe down, you'll be lucky to grow up at all," said Cagney, who had attracted the attention of a particularly inquisitive llama and was having terrifying flashbacks about the last time she'd come so close.

Aidan smiled at his youngest cousin. "Go, but be quick."

Tess skipped towards the tent. She balled her fist to knock, but a low, husky voice from within obviously sensed her presence. "Enter!" came an ethereal voice.

Tess yanked back the flap and found herself in a small, dark space in which someone had wafted way too much incense. On a low, wooden stool, perched an elderly woman, hunched over a table. In the middle of the table sat a glass ball. Tess doubted it was crystal, but it was mighty impressive, nevertheless.

Tess tried her best not to bound. The table looked slightly rickety and she'd hate for the ball to dislodge and roll off. Tess didn't know a lot about telling fortunes, but she had a feeling that destroying a crystal ball would not be the best beginning.

The fortune teller had several scarfs draped over her head and tiny gold pendants covering her forehead. Lifting her arm, the old woman emitted a jangling sound and, with an immaculately manicured fingernail, beckoned Tess towards her.

"Come, little one. Let Madam Marla show you your future."

Tess hurried to the table and pulled out a stool.

Madam Marla held out her hand. Tess grasped it and gave it a good shake. "Ah no, little one. First you must cross my palm with silver."

Tess rifled through several layers of tulle. She came up with a dime, a stamp with Lilibet's head on it and a hair tie. "Sorry, I don't have any silver."

Madam Marla shrugged. "Not many people do. No matter, let us glimpse into your future." The gypsy waved her long delicate hands over the crystal ball. "I see you are not from around here."

"That's right," said Tess, inching forward. "I'm from …"

Madam Marla gave a warning sssh. "I see you are from the New World."

"I am?" asked Tess. "I thought I was from Texas."

"Yes. A world of plenty. A world of family and friends."

"Oh yes," said Tess. "I have plenty of those."

The fortune teller let out another sharp hiss, causing Tess to wonder if Madam Marla had been a librarian in a previous career.

"I see you have a brother! Wait! No, a sister, although, to be honest, it's quite difficult to tell."

Tess' eyes widened.

"And many cousins."

Tess nodded, vigorously.

Madam Marla grasped Tess' sticky hands and flipped them over. "I see a great life ahead." A bright red fingernail traced its way across Tess' palm. "A life filled with love and art and ..."

Tess cocked her head to one side and wrinkled her nose. She had seen those hands before. They were not the hands of an old woman. They were smooth, soft and immaculately tidy.

Tess thought back. This reminded her of something, but what? Tess sniffed, then sniffed again. The smell of incense was fading being replaced by the smell of fresh Cornish pasties and a waft of cinnamon.

Tess scrambled to her feet and made a dash for the exit. Suddenly, it all fell into place. She needed to tell someone, and she needed to tell them now.

39

Competition

Tess barreled out of the tent and straight into Cagney. Bouncing off her cousin's fuzzy back, Tess landed tiara-down on the grass.

"Careful," said Cagney, irritably, "you'll damage my wings."

Aidan rounded the corner and sprung Tess to her feet. "Whatcha doing down there?"

"I ran into Cagney," said Tess.

"She is rather, erm, large," said Aidan, avoiding Cagney's glare.

Tess tugged at the bottom of Aidan's dress. "Where's Olivia and Lissy?"

"Olivia's demolishing those coconuts over there. And Lissy figured out what the tombola is and is throwing a hoop over a rubber duck, but her ruffles are messing up her aim."

Tess started to bounce. "I have to tell you something."

Cagney tried unsuccessfully to arrange her crumpled antenna. "If the fortune teller said you're going to be a fairy when you grow up, I'd ask for my money back."

"She said nothing about fairies," said Tess.

"Same goes for princesses." Cagney hopped up and down, trying to shift a wing. "Ain't gonna happen."

Olivia ambled around the corner. She was almost obliterated by a pink fuzzy teddy bear. "Look what I won."

Tess clutched her hands together and gazed imploringly at her sister.

Olivia frowned. "What?"

Tess gazed harder.

Olivia turned to Aidan. "What does she want?"

Aidan grinned. "I'm assuming she wants the very large, very pink, very fluffy teddy bear. But I could be wrong."

"Oh yeah." Olivia tossed the bear towards Tess. "I was going to give it to you anyway. What would *I* do with something cute?"

"Mind the wings," said Tess and Cagney, simultaneously.

Tess' voice floated up from behind the enormous bear. "Guys, I have to tell you something."

"Look what I won." Lissy rounded the corner swirling a knitted woolen hat around her finger. "It has a couple of holes on either side, but I can easily sew those up."

Cagney gave her cousin's new hat a cursory glance and gave thanks that the wig Lissy currently wore prevented her from modeling it.

"Are you children entering the fancy dress competition?"

The five turned to see Major Puffin approaching. Buckingham, Balmoral and Windsor all straining in Cagney's direction.

"Whatever makes you think that," mumbled Cagney, trying to get some distance between her and the snapping corgis.

"Yes, sir. We're just on our way," said Lissy.

"Guys!" said Tess. "I've got to tell you—"

"Right then," said Major Puffin, trying to stop Windsor from climbing inside Cagney's costume. "Well, leap to it. You wouldn't want to be late now, would you?"

"Heavens no," whispered Cagney, trying to disentangle herself from three leashes wrapped around her luminous yellow legs.

Raising his cane, Major Puffin herded the five towards the stage. Balmoral growled and Buckingham tried to take a few nips out of Cagney's ankles.

"Get off me, you scruffy little mutts!" muttered Cagney.

A Labrador, Lissy had seen in the shaggy dog contest came bounding towards them. She, too, made a beeline for Cagney's fluffy feet.

"Get away," cried Major Puffin, waving his stick and smartly dislodging Aidan's hat.

Everywhere they looked, children and grown-ups flocked towards the stage to be judged. There were mermaids, leprechauns, electrical appliances and even a yeti.

"Hurry along, now," cried Major Puffin. "Seven and under to the left, eight and above to the right."

Tess was herded to the left. Aidan tried to tell her not to leave the area, but in the jumble of wings, tiaras and fluffy tutus, he immediately lost her.

"Boys to the back, girls at the front." Major Puffin stuck out his cane. "Are you a boy or a girl?"

Aidan sighed. "It's the tights, isn't it?"

Puffin jolted in recognition. "Sorry, my boy - didn't recognize you in all that, erm, green."

"That's okay. Could be worse," Aidan nodded towards Cagney.

Major Puffin's eyes widened. "Indeed, my boy, indeed."

Aidan watched Major P. and his three dogs climb the stairs to the stage and tap the microphone. "Testing? Testing?"

"Aww, get on with it man," muttered Basil, who sat at the back of the stage with Henri.

Major P flushed. "My lords, ladies and gentlemen."

"He forgot the pirates," whispered Olivia.

"I would like to welcome you to the sixty-fifth annual Bumble Bottom Fancy Dress Competition."

A spattering of applause rippled through the spectators and several arghs were heard from the pirates.

"I do believe this might be the best turnout yet," said Puffin, the microphone squealing in protest. Puffin staggered backwards and cleared his throat. "And, to judge the fancy dress competition we have the Right Honorable Lord and Lady Featherington-Twit."

Lissy was happy to hear a roar of approval. She was not surprised the Twits were popular. How could they not be?

Aidan surveyed the crowd. It was like a zoo, except far less organized. He searched for the girls. Lissy was being jostled by a wide-screen TV, while Olivia was trying to wedge herself between a purple bunny and the planet Saturn. Only Cagney seemed unjostled; *must be the smell,* thought Aidan.

Lissy got in line ahead of Bo Peep and a fluffy lamb. It sounded like there would be some kind of parade and then the judging would begin. Good, then they could get back to the Googly Gherkin and, with any luck, track down Rupert.

The wide-screen TV took a step back and landed on Lissy's shoe, which gave off an embarrassing squeak. *In the name of Great Aunt Maud, would this never end?*

Olivia was not having fun. If one more person pulled or stood on her tail, she would go find one of those coconuts and do some serious damage.

The line finally moved. She could see Lissy several pirates ahead. Jeesh, these people really had a thing for pirates. It wasn't like they were anywhere near the sea. Yes, Bumble Bottom had a duck pond, but it was hardly the final frontier in naval activity.

Olivia caught the eye of Lord Featherington-Twit. His brow creased and he looked puzzled. Cagney joined the back of the line and vowed she would be a better person if she was just allowed to go back to the Googly Gherkin without another dog nipping her ankles.

Waddling along, she saw Henri bustling towards her. She plastered a half-sincere smile on her face and tried not to seem petulant. Henri and Basil had been really good to them. Even Cagney could admit that.

Henri poked her gigantic tummy. "I say, what on earth are you wearing?"

Cagney tried to look down, but it wasn't worth the struggle. "I'm not sure, I think it's some kind of mutant ... wait, what did you say?"

"I said, what are you wearing?"

"The costume?" asked Cagney, confused.

"Well, I can see that, my dear. The question is, *why* are you wearing that, erm, costume?"

Cagney stopped and was promptly bumped into by a jar of peanut butter. Cagney stepped aside for the jar to go around and grabbed Henri's arm. "But *you* gave us these costumes. Sally told us."

"I don't think so, my dear. I think Sally has played a bit of a joke on you."

Cagney stood dumbfounded. *If the Featherington-Twits didn't leave them the costumes, then why did Sally say they did?*

Cagney started to waddle faster, but she was boxed in by an eight-year-old Snow White and a bumper-sized packet of crayons.

She needed to find Lissy or, in a pinch, Olivia. Something didn't add up. Sally had tricked them into wearing these ridiculous costumes and Sally would pay.

Ahead in the crowd she saw Olivia's floppy ears. Cagney barged her way to the front of the line, grabbed Olivia by her tail and dragged her towards the large red wig, bobbing several pirates ahead.

"If you don't let go of my ..."

"Ah, put a cork in it," said Cagney. "It's the costumes. They weren't from the Twits."

The large ball of red hair spun around. "You mean Sally lied?" said Lissy.

"Why would she do that?" asked Olivia.

Lissy took off her nose, which immediately let out a squeak. "To get us away from the Googly Gherkin, of course."

"But why? That makes no sense," said Cagney.

"Nothing makes any sense," said Lissy.

"I'll tell you what doesn't make any sense," said Aidan, emerging from behind a rather stout Alice in Wonderland.

Alice jumped back as Aidan's bow nabbed her sharply on the shins.

Lissy saw the look of panic on Aidan's face. "What's wrong?"

Aidan removed his mask and took a deep breath. "It's Tess. She's disappeared."

40

Missing

A re you sure?" Lissy watched several fairies skip by. "It's really crowded and, let's be honest, for once, she's not the strangest dressed person within a fifty-mile radius."

"I'm sure," said Aidan. "Lord Featherington-Twit said he saw a Chinese fairy and a large pink teddy bear running across the green. Well, the teddy bear wasn't running, but you get what I mean."

"Couldn't have been her," said Olivia. "Tess never runs. She skips, twirls and occasionally canters but she definitely doesn't run."

"Well, according to F-T, he was having a perfectly normal conversation with her one second, and the next thing he knows, she's flying across the grass, wings a-flapping."

"It's true," said Basil, joining the cousins. "I would have gone after her, but I got jostled by an indignant mermaid and by the time I retrieved my hat, she'd gone."

"Gone where?" asked Lissy.

"The obvious choice is the Googly Gherkin," suggested Aidan.

"'Fraid not," said Basil." She tore off in completely the opposite direction."

"What were you talking about, sir?" said Lissy, trying not to squeak.

"I just complimented her on her charming fairy costume and asked where she got it."

"She's a smart cookie, that sister of yours." Lissy turned to Olivia. "She figured it out before we did."

"Figured out what?" asked Olivia.

"That these costumes were not left for us by the Featherington-Twits," said Lissy.

"Oh, certainly not," said Basil. "Wouldn't have thought you were the type."

"We're not," said Olivia, loosening her collar.

"Did she not give you *any* clue where she was going?" asked Lissy.

Basil took off his straw boater and scratched what was left of his hair. "Not exactly, but she got very excited about fingernails."

"Fingernails?" exclaimed Cagney.

"Red ones and dirty ones."

"He's lost it," Cagney muttered.

"My dear young lady, it is true I have lost many things in my life, including a rather fine dachshund named Lionel, but I have not lost my mind."

"The fortune teller!" exclaimed Aidan. "That's when Tess said she needed to tell us something."

"And we didn't listen to her." Lissy shook her head, but quickly thought better of it.

"Grandma's not going to be pleased if we lose Tess … again," said Aidan.

"My parents won't be exactly thrilled either," said Olivia. "Why on earth couldn't she stay where she was told?"

"Since when has Tess *ever* done what she was told?" said Aidan.

Olivia shrugged. "You have a point."

"Enough! We have to find her. Let's split into pairs. Aidan and Olivia, you head in the direction

Tess went. Cagney and I will go see the fortune teller."

"And I'll wander back to the Googly Gherkin and see if she's turned up there, shall I?" said Lord Featherington-Twit. "I'll tell Henri what's happened and she can stay here and keep an eye out for her."

"That would be very helpful," said Lissy. "Thank you, sir."

"Okay," said Aidan. "Sounds like a plan. We'll meet back here in twenty minutes and hopefully…" Aidan readjusted his skirt, "one of us will have found a Chinese fairy."

The microphone crackled to life. A squeak filled the air.

"It wasn't me. I didn't move," said Lissy.

Cagney rolled her eyes. "It's Puffin and that darn microphone."

Major Puffin continued to drone in the background "And the winner of the boys seven and under…"

"Twenty minutes should be enough. See you back here when the clock strikes half past," said Aidan, checking his watch.

A boy, around five, dressed as a red and white straw, attempted to hop onto the stage.

"Yes, and if you see Mr. Smythe, for goodness sake, one of you stay with him," said Lissy.

"And the winner of the girls seven and above is … now, where did I put it?"

Aidan saluted Lissy and knocked off his hat. He bent to pick it up and smacked Olivia in the stomach with his bow.

"Ow," said Olivia, "mind where you're putting that thing, it's dangerous."

People were starting to sshh them. Cagney shushed back.

Lissy bent forward to pick up the hat, when another squeak rang out. She paused mid-stretch. "Okay, that time it was me."

Aidan grasped the feathered hat and shoved it on top of his head.

There was a blur of beige and Cagney looked down to see three snapping corgis at her ankles. "Run for it!" shouted Lissy.

Cagney gave her a look.

"Okay, waddle as fast as you can." Lissy swept up the corgis' leashes and handed them to a startled porcupine.

Staggering backwards, Cagney sidestepped an overripe banana and tottered away from the stage. The microphone crackled to life. Darth Vader put a hand on Cagney's fuzzy shoulder. "Young lady. Come back. You've won!"

41

Confusion

Cagney kept waddling until she was sure she was out of sight. *Now, where was that fortune teller?*

Cagney heard a squeak. Turning, she saw Lissy lumbering towards her.

Lissy put her neck frill back into position and grinned. "I'm surprised you could run that fast."

Cagney sniffed the air. "Do I really smell that bad?"

"Olivia's smelled worse, but not by much." Lissy scanned the crowd. "Look, there's the fortune teller booth. I guess we'd better check inside."

"If we have to." Cagney sidled towards the tent, pulled aside the flap and wedged herself through the gap.

"I can't believe Cagney won the fancy dress competition," said Aidan.

Olivia's dimple deepened. "Yeah, that'll be one for the record books."

"How long have they been having these competitions? Coz I bet that's the first time the winner did a runner," said Aidan.

Olivia grinned. "Yep, you're getting more English every day. Soon you're going to sound like Lilibet."

"Am not." Aidan scowled. "I may be wearing a skirt, but I do *not* sound like a girl."

"That reminds me," said Olivia. "When we get back to the Googly Gherkin I want you to look something up in that rhyming slang book that Billy gave you."

The two cousins stood by the Maypole. Several girls with flowers in their hair were busy prancing around it. The ribbons in their outstretched hands, made a colorful pattern around the pole. To the left, the Morris Men were warming up, ready to start jingling.

"It's hopeless," said Aidan. "We're never going to find her."

"There's too many people," said Olivia. "My mom is officially going to kill me - again." Aidan smiled. Olivia presented a hard exterior, but under it all he was sure she had a heart of gold. Pretty sure, at least.

Olivia saw a splash of pink in the crowd and whipped around. Her tail hit Aidan smartly on the shins. A five-year-old Pink Panther ambled by. Olivia's shoulders sagged.

"There she is!" Aidan grabbed Olivia's leash.

Olivia spun around but stopped dead in her tracks. "Who's that with her? And why are they dragging her along by the wings?"

Olivia and Aidan locked eyes. Without saying a word, they took off across the green.

"Hello, anyone here?" said Lissy, fumbling through the dark.

"Welcome to the wonderful world of…"

Cagney took a step towards the crystal ball. "Actually, we're here because we've lost someone."

Madam Marla beckoned Cagney and Lissy towards her with a long red fingernail. "Those who are lost, we will find," she chanted.

Cagney didn't know where Madam Marla's accent was from, but she had once seen a movie set in Eastern Europe and this sounded suspiciously similar.

The fortune teller bent her bejeweled head low and twirled her fingers over the crystal ball. Lissy sidled up behind Cagney. "Look at the fingernails," she whispered.

Cagney squinted at the fingers doing some kind of dance over the crystal ball. "Okay lady, what have you done with our cousin?"

In one decisive shuffle, Cagney reached across the table and grabbed Madam Marla's hands. Startled, the fortune teller lurched backwards and, forgetting she was sitting on a low stool, toppled onto the grass.

"Oops!" said Cagney.

Lissy squeaked her way around the table and stared down at the mass of skirts, scarfs and sequins. Madam Marla's headscarf was dislodged, and so was a long gray wig. Rising, the fortune teller made a valiant effort to re-adjust her petticoats, but it was too late.

Lissy peered into the gloom and gasped. "It's you!"

Aidan could see Olivia ahead of him. She had barreled through the Maypole dance and narrowly missed being clonked on the head by an overly enthusiastic Morris Man. Olivia's middle name began with an R. Aidan couldn't remember what it was - probably something Chinese - but right now he was pretty sure it stood for reckless.

Taking a more circuitous route, Aidan was close on her heels. Olivia was like a hound dog on the scent - literally; with her tail wagging back and forth, she left a trail of carnage in her wake.

He could see Tess ahead, being led firmly across the green. Aidan hated to raise his voice, but it seemed acceptable given the situation. He opened his mouth to yell, but Olivia beat him to it.

With a voice worthy of an Army sergeant, Olivia screamed her sister's name.

"Hello, hello, hello!" Olivia skidded to a halt inches from the dark blue uniform of P.C. Pickle. "What's going on here, then?" said the policeman.

Olivia tried to sidestep the constable, but Inspector Watts appeared out of nowhere and grabbed her by the floppy ears. "I believe you have some explaining to do, young man."

It was only with slight relief that Aidan realized Inspector Watts was talking to Olivia and not him.

"Let me go," said Olivia, squirming.

"I don't think so, laddy. Look at the mess you've made." Inspector Watts spun Olivia around.

The Maypole dancers had become a tangled mess, three of the Morris Men were piled on the ground, and the winner of the shaggy dog competition was whimpering behind a scarecrow.

Olivia took a deep breath. "I didn't mean to. I just need to get my sister." Olivia swiveled around, searching for where she had last seen Tess, but Tess had vanished, she was gone and furthermore, she was not there.

"And why is that?" asked Inspector Watts.

Aiden stepped forward before Olivia could get herself in any more trouble. "We're sorry, sir. It's just my cousin, she's only six, and right now it looks like she's being kidnapped."

Lissy hauled the fortune teller to her feet. Beads lay scattered across the grass and a gaping hole billowed from where Lissy's oversized shoes had torn her gown. The amazing Madam Marla did not look happy. In fact, she looked down right mad. With her wig askew and her makeup smudged, she didn't seem all that amazing, either.

"What do you think you're playing at?"

All traces of the thick European accent had disappeared, replaced by the crisp tones of Penelope, the librarian.

"You're not Madam Marla," said Lissy, letting go of her hand.

"Not exactly," said Penelope, adjusting her wig in what was obviously a losing battle.

"Not at all," said Cagney.

"You've got as much Romany blood as *I've* got," said Lissy, indignantly.

"All right, all right." Penelope righted the stool and perched on top. "There's not a lot to it. You just wave your hands around and tell them what they want to hear. It's normally to do with love."

"Tess asked you about love?" said Lissy, horrified.

"Is she the small Chinese child that normally resembles forty-pounds of cotton candy?"

"Yep," said Lissy and Cagney, simultaneously.

"No, we talked about ..." Penelope scratched her wayward wig. "Now, what *did* we talk about?"

"If we could move this along," said Cagney. "It's *slightly* important."

"Why don't you ask her yourself?"

Lissy sank onto the ground and plopped her white-painted face into her hands. "We can't. She's missing."

"Kidnapped?" Inspector Watts scrunched down on one knee and held Olivia by the shoulders. "What are you talking about, son? I think you'd better start at the beginning and tell me everything."

"Everything?" said Olivia, appalled. She eyeballed Aidan and minutely shook her head. "You'll never believe us."

Inspector Watts rose to his feet. "Just try me."

"It all started when we went into Odds and Ends," said Aidan.

Olivia gritted her teeth. *What part of 'no' did Aidan not get?*

Aidan ran through the strange course of events occurring since their arrival. Quickly and efficiently he filled the policemen in, thankfully leaving out all mention of white ladies, guns and badgers.

Aidan took a breath. "Anyhow, our plan was to follow Rupert ... and Cagney did a good job, until she fell into a pigsty."

"Then Sally told us Lord and Lady Featherington-Twit left us these, erm, costumes," said Olivia, straining to get away from Inspector Watts' firm grip.

"And they've been so kind," said Aidan. "We didn't feel we could let them down."

"I see," said Inspector Watts. "This is all fascinating, but what does it have to do with your sister being kidnapped?"

"It has *everything* to do with it," said Aidan. "She was trying to tell us something."

"Yeah, she can be annoying like that sometimes," said Olivia.

"But we didn't listen, and then we see her in the grip of ... well, you know," said Aidan, not exactly sure what description to use.

"I wouldn't worry too much," said P.C. Pickle.

"My six-year-old sister has gone missing, last seen in the clutches of some, some ..." Like Aidan, Olivia struggled for the right word.

The two policemen exchanged glances.

"Let's just go look for them, shall we?" said Inspector Watts. "Come on now, they can't have gone *too* far."

The church clock struck the half-hour.

"Ah shoot," said Aidan, "we're late."

Cagney, Lissy and Penelope stood by the stage and waited. The crowds of children had dispersed and it seemed like the next competition was about to start.

Cagney tapped her toe, a sure sign she was annoyed. Lissy didn't dare tap hers. Penelope was already giving her sidelong glances and she couldn't be bothered to explain about the squeaking. Lissy spotted Aidan and Olivia tearing towards them.

Then she spotted D.I. Watts and P.C. Pickle close on their tail.

"Oh lord," said Lissy, removing her nose, "what have they done now?"

Cagney tried to cross her arms but failed. "I hope Olivia didn't go and beat anyone up again."

"Your cousin beats people up?" asked Penelope.

"She doesn't mean to," said Lissy. "At least, I don't think she does. It's just people tend to get damaged around her."

"Sorry we're late," said Aidan, skidding to a halt.

"Yeah," said Olivia. "We got a little delayed." She glanced at P.C. Pickle, who had staggered up behind them, laying a bony hand on Olivia's shoulder.

"Oh God, you've been arrested," said Cagney, who had always feared having a felon in the family.

"What?" said Olivia, shrugging off the hand. "I haven't been arrested! Not yet, anyway."

P.C. Pickle pointed his finger towards Olivia and gave it a good shake. "Although given the amount of damage you did, we might think about reckless endangerment."

Lissy caught Penelope's eye. "Told ya."

"Why's she here?" Olivia whispered to Lissy, seeing Penelope for the first time.

"She's the fortune teller," explained Lissy.

"Your brother, here, told me all about Mr. Smythe. Quite a bit of detective work, if I do say so myself," said Inspector Watts.

Cagney almost smiled, but the sun had made an appearance, and her costume was starting to stink. She settled on a grimace.

Lissy pointed across the green. "She's over there."

Olivia spun around and scanned the crowd for Tess. But it wasn't Tess Lissy was pointing at. It was Sally.

42

Narnia

"You kids head back to the Googly Gherkin," said Inspector Watts. "I think we need to have a little word with Miss Bishop."

"Don't worry," said P.C. Pickle, smiling. "We'll meet you there, and if your sister hasn't shown up by then, we'll start searching a little harder."

"Come on," said Cagney. "Let's get out of these ridiculous costumes and then we can figure out what we're going to do about Tess."

The fête was still going strong as the four plodded across the green. As they approached the Googly Gherkin, Lord Featherington-Twit could be seen on the picnic benches, his long legs stretched out, his hat twirling nervously in his hands.

"Ah, there you are. No sign, I'm afraid. I did try all your rooms, but the only person up there was that Odds and Ends man, said he was looking for Sally."

Olivia kicked the picnic bench. "Great, just great."

Featherington-Twit rose to his feet. "I'll be getting back - got to judge the best-dressed scarecrow competition, but I'll keep an eye out, as it were."

Inside the Googly Gherkin, the four trudged up the stairs and along the dimly lit hallway.

"Dibs on using the bathroom first." Cagney muscled Lissy out of the way and grabbed the door handle. "Great, there's someone inside."

"Maybe it's Smythe," whispered Aidan.

Cagney pressed her ear to the door. Someone was singing off-key. Way off.

"I recognize that voice," said Olivia.

"Yeah," said Lissy. "So do I."

Olivia pressed her eye against the keyhole. There was movement within, but the keyhole was blurry, not to mention miniscule.

The singing was replaced by a crinkling sound.

"What's that?" asked Aidan, leaning in.

The door lurched open and the four flew forward, landing in a heap next to ten sparkly pink toenails. In a pink fluffy bathrobe, holding a bumper bag of Hula Hoops stood Tess.

Aidan threw his hat onto the bed and inspected his legs. They were still itchy, even minus the tights. The cousins had taken a few minutes to change and Olivia and Tess' bed was crowded with costumes. At one end lay Aidan's Robin Hood outfit, next to it a black and white puppy dog suit. Lissy's clown costume lay discarded and squeakless and, at the end, Tess had tossed a fairy tutu, tiara and wings.

Cagney burst through the door and aimed her psychedelic bumble bee outfit onto the pile. She turned and regarded the others. "I say we never mention this again."

Aidan nodded.

"What happens in England, stays in England," said Olivia.

Lissy turned to Tess. "You disappeared."

Tess pushed the costumes to one side and launched herself onto the bed. "Well, technically I…"

"You left the competition," said Aidan.

"You were being manhandled by that, that … manhandler," said Olivia.

"Manhandled?" said Tess, surprised. "There was no man handling me."

"But we saw you," said Aidan.

"And then Cagney got chased by dogs and Olivia wrecked the Maypole dance," said Lissy.

Olivia scowled. "And then Aidan blurted everything out to the police. They probably think we're a complete bunch of idiots."

Lissy sighed. "Won't be the first time."

Aidan shook his head. "It probably won't be the last."

"Tess, you can't just run off and not tell anyone." Lissy scooted Tess over and perched beside her. "We were worried about you."

"But I didn't run off. I told Lord Featherington-Twit where I was going."

"You did?" asked Aidan. "He doesn't seem to remember that part. He seems to remember you going on about fingernails."

"I was trying to explain—"

"Hey!" Olivia approached the large freestanding wardrobe.

Aidan stopped scratching his legs and glanced up. "What?"

"The wardrobe, or whatever these Brits call closets, it's different."

"It's a solid huge chunk of wood with a door," said Cagney. "How different can it be?"

"It's moved," said Olivia.

Lissy slid off the bed. "She's right. Look at the floor. The wood here's all scratched up."

Aidan stopped itching and came to join them. "That's strange. I wonder who moved it?"

Cagney pushed her cousins out the way and started to feel along the base of the wardrobe. "Maybe *this* leads to the Turnip room."

"Turpin," corrected Lissy.

"Or Narnia," said Tess.

Cagney snorted.

Aidan's eyes lit up. "Check inside."

Cagney rolled her eyes. "Tell me you don't think Narnia lies through there?"

"Of course not," said Aidan, sheepishly. "But it doesn't hurt to check."

Olivia twisted the handle and the wardrobe creaked open. Everyone leaned forward. There was a scratching noise and something amongst the masses of pink clothing moved.

Olivia pulled aside one of Tess' many ruffled dress and stuck her head into the wardrobe. The scratching came again.

"What is it?" asked Cagney.

"A secret passage?" squealed Lissy.

"A hiding space?" suggested Aidan.

"No!" Olivia turned. In cupped hands she grasped a tiny creature. "It's a mouse."

Cagney let out a blood-curdling scream, stopped, then produced another.

"Should I slap her?" asked Tess.

Olivia studied the small ball of fur in her hands. "I'd do it for you, but I don't want to drop Mickey."

Cagney drew in a third breath and Aidan drew back his arm. But, Lissy beat him to it. A sharp crack resonated through the air.

"We don't want her to hyperventilate," said Lissy, suppressing a grin. She winked at Aidan. "Plus she'd never forgive you."

"Who says I'm going to forgive *you?*" asked Cagney, glaring.

Tess shimmied the window up and Olivia placed the tiny mouse on the ledge below.

When she turned, Lissy's bottom was sticking out the wardrobe. "What are you doing?"

"What do you *think* I'm doing?"

"You know, she's getting very sassy," said Olivia, wiping her hands on the back of Aidan's tee.

"I'm looking to see if there's a secret bottom or a false back or a ..." Lissy's voice trailed off as her head disappeared further inside the wardrobe.

"Did you find anything?" asked Aidan, coming to join Lissy.

"Here, move over," said Olivia, shifting her cousins to the side.

"Maybe it's the drawer at the top." Aidan put a foot on the bottom ridge and hoisted himself skyward. Grabbing the handle, he flung the drawer upwards and peeked inside.

"That thing is going to topple forward and squish you like a bag of socks," said Cagney. "Guys, I'm telling you, you need some counterbalance and Tess' tutus, extensive though they are, are not going to cut it."

"What?" said Olivia, Lissy and Aidan, simultaneously.

Cagney snuck a look at the windowsill. The mouse had disappeared. She yanked the window closed, causing a gust of air to sweep the room. Spinning around, Cagney stifled yet another scream.

Silently, the wardrobe had swung forward, but not as she had predicted by toppling over. Instead,

the entire wardrobe had shifted like one enormous
door, revealing a gaping hole behind it.

43

Secret Passageway

"Oops," said Tess.

Aidan leapt from the wardrobe. Startled by the movement, Olivia and Lissy withdrew their heads.

"Was it an earthquake?" asked Olivia.

"I don't think England has earthquakes," said Lissy.

"Then how did the wardrobe get over here?" asked Aidan.

"It wasn't me," said Tess, backing away from the wall. "At least, I'm pretty sure it wasn't me."

"Really?" said Olivia. "Just like the time it wasn't you when the car jumped into neutral and rolled down the driveway?"

Tess nodded, enthusiastically. "Exactly like that time."

Lissy clambered out the wardrobe. "What did you do, Tess?"

"I pressed this." Tess pointed to a small lever, which previously lay camouflaged. "I wondered what it did. I sure didn't expect it to do that."

"And I'm betting she didn't expect it to reveal a hidden window, either," said Cagney, moving towards the opening.

"A what?" said the others together.

"Yes, Harry Potter, here, has found the secret chamber," said Cagney.

Aidan, Lissy and Olivia all stuck their heads around the side of the wardrobe. One by one their mouths dropped open.

"I don't know why you're so surprised," said Cagney. "It *is* England. I mean, if this were Texas then yep, we'd have a major tourist attraction. But heck, this is England. Hidden passageways are practically built into the architectural plans."

Olivia moved towards the opening. It was squat and square and sat about two feet off the floor.

Scratched into a dark wood frame were the words 'George's Door.'

Tess shuddered. "I sure hope there's not a dragon in there."

Olivia brushed back a cobweb and poked her head farther into the hole.

"What do you see?" asked Cagney.

"It's hard to tell." Olivia withdrew her head. "Can someone fetch my..."

Aidan slapped a flashlight into her palm.

"Thanks." Olivia flipped the switch and shone the beam into the hole.

"What's there?" asked Lissy.

Olivia hoisted herself onto the ledge. Rising to a crouching position, she shuffled to the side and disappeared. A second later her head reappeared at the top of the frame. "It's a staircase."

Aidan moved forward and gingerly brushed away the remaining cobwebs. Sitting on the ledge, he swung his legs up before scrambling to his feet and disappearing behind the wall.

Lissy shrugged. "I guess we might as well."

Tess was already scampering through the hole.

Lissy turned to Cagney. "Are you coming?"

Cagney sighed. The thought of missing any discoveries was too much to bear. "If I have to."

By the time Cagney scrambled through the hole, Olivia had ascended several steep steps. She was beginning to think this was a waste of time when suddenly the stairs stopped. Olivia reached out and discovered a solid surface. She shone the flashlight upward and could just make out an old-fashioned latch.

Flipping the latch upward, she pushed, causing a door to swing open. The last thing she saw was a large room, before the flashlight flickered and died.

"Who turned the light out?" asked Tess.

"It's the flashlight." Olivia tapped the cylinder in her palm, but it made no difference. The flashlight had run out of flash.

By this time, Aidan and Lissy had stumbled through the doorway behind her. Aidan reached backwards, and finding Tess' hand, helped her the last couple of steps while holding the door open for his sister.

The room was dark, very dark. Knowing from experience to let the darkness settle before attempting to move, the five stood still and listened.

Tess slipped her hand into Aidan's. She wasn't afraid of the dark, but felt better knowing Aidan stood beside her.

Olivia's foot touched an empty jar; a jar, from the smell of it, that had once contained pickles.

There was a squeak from behind their heads and some rustling. Cagney wished she'd stayed downstairs. Where there was one mouse there were bound to be others. The whole attic was probably riddled with them.

Cagney shivered, but then she heard another sound coming from the opposite direction. The noise grew louder, a rat maybe? And then she heard some kind of gurgling noise? "Tess, is that your stomach?"

Tess looked down and checked for signs of gurgling.

"I don't think that's Tess," said Olivia.

"Not unless she's projecting from the other side of the room," said Lissy.

"Then what is it?" Aidan felt the hairs on the back of his neck prickle.

"It might be my imagination, but it sounds like someone snoring," said Tess.

The five listened as another gurgle, louder this time, erupted from somewhere too close for comfort.

"I don't like it," said Lissy. "I'm going back."

"I'll show you the way," said Tess, turning.

"Something's moving," said Olivia, squinting into the darkness.

"It's a rat," said Cagney, hastening backwards.

"It's too big for a rodent," said Olivia, moving closer.

"Not helpful," said Cagney, wrestling with Lissy to find the door latch.

"Maybe a cat?" suggested Aidan, who thought it only gentlemanly to help his cousins find the exit.

Olivia scolded herself for not checking the flashlight batteries. At least her eyes were adjusting to the dark. Taking another step forward, she began to see the outline of an old-fashioned bed frame. The bed lay heaped with blankets and, if it hadn't been situated in a secret room at the top of a hidden staircase, would have looked quite snuggly.

It was when Olivia thought she'd never locate the source of the noise that the bedclothes started to move.

Olivia took a step back. Then another. A figure in an oversized men's shirt with a large feathered hat on his head rose from the bedclothes. Olivia closed her eyes, then opened them again. Olivia wasn't shocked easily but, if she wasn't mistaken, standing in front of her loomed the ghost of Dick Turpin.

*
*   *
*   *

44

Dick Turpin

Olivia blinked. She blinked again. Nope, there was definitely a ghost in front of her.

She wondered if she'd done more damage than she'd realized when she'd fallen out the window.

As these thoughts tumbled through her mind she heard the scream - then another, then a third. She guessed the others had finally seen what she saw. Olivia turned. Cagney, Lissy and Tess all stood, their mouths cavernous. It was hard to tell who was screaming the loudest. If there was an Olympic event for synchronized screaming, her cousins would definitely have a fighting chance at gold.

Olivia turned back towards the apparition and realized it was getting nearer. She felt a hand on her shoulder and jumped. Aidan pulled her back towards him. At that moment there was a rush for the door. Olivia watched as Lissy, Cagney and Tess all tried to squeeze through at the same time. Tess, the smallest, managed to slip through first. Cagney was next, quickly followed by Lissy. One of them still screamed, but it was unclear, at this point, which one.

Olivia locked eyes with Aidan and the two of them turned and fled. Not bothering to shut the door behind them, Olivia half tumbled, half slipped down the narrow staircase. She could feel Aidan close behind; at least she hoped it was Aidan. Reaching the bottom, she scrambled through the hole and into the bedroom. Aidan appeared seconds later.

"Quick!" said Cagney, flapping her hand towards the wardrobe. "Push it back!"

Lissy, Olivia and Aidan rushed to the front of the wardrobe and started to shove. The wardrobe swung back and clicked into place.

The three slid to the ground, their faces flushed, their hearts hammering.

"I don't like it," said Lissy. "I don't like it one bit. Ghosts are pretend. They're made up to scare little kids."

"Well, I don't know about you ..." Aidan wiped a bead of sweat from his forehead. "But this kid is truly scared."

Cagney paced the room. "Can't ghosts come through walls?"

Aidan and Lissy exchanged glances.

Olivia had her head in her hands, her knees pulled up close to her chest. Suddenly she slid forward. "Stop it."

"Stop what?" asked Cagney.

"Lissy's pushing me."

"No I'm not," said Lissy.

"Now she's pushing me," said Aidan.

Lissy raised her hands. "I'm not pushing either of you."

"So, why am I moving?" asked Olivia.

Aidan glanced from left to right. All three of them were inching forward.

Cagney let out another blood-curdling scream. Pointing towards the wardrobe, she teetered backwards and straight into a chair, which pitched backwards, landing with a thump on the floorboards.

Olivia scrambled forward in time to see a hand protruding from the hole in the wall.

Leaping to her feet, Olivia started to push the wardrobe back. Realizing what was happening, Aidan and Lissy joined her.

"Cagney, come help." Lissy peeked around the side of the wardrobe. Cagney's legs stuck bolt upright. Her eyes were wide as saucers and all color had drained from her face. She really did look like she'd seen a ghost. It was not comforting.

Olivia pushed harder, but it was no good; they were losing ground, slowly slipping backwards on the wooden floor. Olivia saw the arm of a white linen shirt appear. A door slammed behind them. Darn Cagney, she was bigger than all of them and she'd chosen this moment to run. Maybe that wasn't such a bad idea. They were fighting a losing battle as the wardrobe gave another couple of inches.

"This is hopeless," said Aidan. "Cagney, come help us!"

Olivia's head snapped towards the door. *So it wasn't Cagney who'd left. It was Tess. Dang! Maybe Tess had the right idea.*

"I think we should make a run for it," said Aidan.

Olivia and Lissy both nodded.

"All right," said Aidan, "on the count of three. One, two ..."

"Wait! Are we letting go on three or after three?" asked Lissy.

"Does it matter?" asked Olivia, sweat trickling down her neck.

"Yes it matters," said Lissy. "You let go before me and I'm going to end up splattered against the wall."

"She has a point," said Aidan.

"Oh for goodness sake," said Cagney, who'd hauled herself out of the upturned chair and was edging towards the door. "Just let go!"

Lissy needed no further encouragement. She grabbed Olivia and Aidan's hands and pulled them with her. With the weight removed, the wardrobe burst forward. Hunched in the wall opening stood the figure of Dick Turpin.

Lissy gulped. In the attic she had only imagined how terrifying he was. In the reality of daylight her imagination was proved correct and then some.

The pale figure let out a moan and Lissy felt Aidan push her behind him. The ghost seemed to be heading for the door. Surely he wouldn't venture into a crowded bar? As far as Lissy knew, ghosts liked to scare people. There was no need to take it any farther - he was doing a mighty fine job right here.

Lissy felt her back hit a solid surface. Reaching out, she felt for the doorknob. Something cool and clammy grasped her wrist. She let out a piercing shriek.

"Stop your screaming, it's only me," said Cagney. "I can't find the handle."

"Turn around and look for it," suggested Lissy.

"*You* turn around and look for it," said Cagney, whose eyes were locked onto the figure emerging from the hole in the wall.

Wearing a pointy three-sided hat, a heavy scarlet coat and knee-high leather boots, he looked identical to the drawings in the library book. The man looked like he'd posed for the pictures himself.

Raising his arms to shoulder level, the ghost planted a step towards them. The floor protested with an almighty creak.

Lissy's fingers stopped searching for the handle. Her brow furrowed.

"What are you waiting for?" asked Cagney. "One of you open the door."

"Wait a second," said Lissy. "Ghosts shouldn't make floors creak."

"And they don't snore," said Aidan, frowning.

"And they don't have the remains of Tess' Cornish pastie down their jacket either," said Olivia.

Cagney stopped fumbling for the way out. "What?"

The ghost took another step forward and oohed.

"You're not a ghost," said Lissy.

"He looks like a ghost," said Cagney.

The apparition lowered his arms, dropped the slow-motion shuffle and bolted towards the window.

"Where's he going?" asked Cagney.

Dick Turpin shimmied the window up about six inches and shoved a leather-clad leg onto the ledge below.

"Should we stop him?" asked Aidan.

"Are you joking?" said Cagney. "We've just spent the last five minutes trying to get away from him. Now he's trying to get away from us. I say let him."

"He doesn't seem to be doing very well," said Aidan, watching as Dick tried to slither through the narrow gap.

Olivia smirked. "I think he's stuck."

Suddenly the door behind them flew open. Tess stood in the hallway. She grinned. "I fetched help."

The cousins heard footsteps pounding down the corridor. Tess stepped aside and revealed the disheveled tramp.

Seeing Potty Potts in the doorway, Dick Turpin made one final dash for freedom, but Potts lunged for the window and grabbed hold of a leather boot.

"I don't think so, laddy," said Potts to the struggling figure, sounding nothing like his former self.

Olivia followed him and grabbed Dick by the collar. Tess lurched forward and held onto his jacket pocket. With a loud rip, Tess teetered backwards as the pocket gave way and an intricate gold ball, a little larger than an orange, tumbled onto the floor.

*
* *
*

45

Explanations

Major Puffin and the F-Ts sat at one side of the table. Seated opposite were Sally, the cousins, various dogs and a very large, very pink fluffy bear. P.C. Pickle, Inspector Watts, plus a third man, introduced as Sergeant Carter sat at either end.

Carrington had just disappeared back into the castle and Henri placed the refilled teapot back on the table. The pot was shrouded in a wooly type of vest that Henri had explained was to keep the tea warm.

Lissy eyed the teapot suspiciously. A second later Lissy took off her own wooly hat, the mystery of the two holes explained - she hadn't won a hat at the fête, she'd won what the English called a tea cosy and she'd been wearing it on her head!

Henri settled back into her wicker chair with a contented sigh. The evening was uncharacteristically warm and, with her back to the balustrade, Henri's white hair resembled a halo, silhouetted by the sun's dying rays. Tess bit into her fifth scone and threw a current to Windsor, or was it Balmoral? To be honest, she couldn't really tell.

Three hours had passed since Potty Potts had arrested Dick Turpin and Inspector Watts had taken Roger Smythe in for questioning.

Inspector Watts put down his teacup and turned to face Tess. "So, tell me, young lady, how did you figure out who Potts was?"

Tess turned her attention to Sergeant Carter. "It was when I got my fortune told. Penelope's nails made me realize what was wrong. There she was, all dressed up as an old gypsy woman, but her hands were the hands of a young woman."

"She's not that young," said Sally, dunking a chocolate biscuit in her tea.

Tess continued. "And her nails were so shiny and clean, and then it hit me. Potty Potts' nails were clean too. When we saw him after being arrested, most of him was filthy, but his nails were trimmed and cared for."

"You noticed his nails?" asked P.C. Pickle, obviously impressed.

Tess nodded. "And I also noticed when you first came to the Googly Gherkin there were three policemen. After Potts was arrested, there were only two."

"Darn good show," said Basil.

"Blimey!" said P.C. Pickle.

"You are a very observant little girl," said Inspector Watts. "Have you given any thought to a career in law enforcement?"

Tess swallowed a gulp of scone. "I'm six. Right now I want to be a fairy."

"Foiled by a fairy," said Sergeant Carter, smiling. "I'll never live it down."

"I say, but how did you figure out Potts was a policeman?" asked Henri.

Tess grinned. "I noticed wherever Mr. Smythe went, Potts wasn't far behind. Pretty soon I realized we weren't the only ones following him. And, if Potts was following him, then there must be a reason."

"She's right," said Sergeant Carter. "My orders were to keep Smythe in sight at all times."

"We'd been concerned about him for quite a while and wanted to keep a closer eye on him. We figured it would be suspicious if a newcomer arrived in the village," said Inspector Watts. "So, when Potts was arrested we substituted one of our own. Carter, here, is about the same size as Potts and we figured no one ever looks at the village tramp. We thought no one would be the wiser."

"No one except a six-year-old fairy," said Basil.

"When I figured out the costumes weren't left by the Featherington-Twits I knew I had to tell someone," said Tess. "I couldn't find P.C. Pickle or Inspector Watts, so I told Potts. I knew by then he was the third policeman."

"So that's why you were running across the green with him," said Olivia.

Tess nodded. "He'd just gone to find Inspector Watts when you guys found me in the bathroom."

"Had you suspected Smythe for long?" asked Henri.

Inspector Watts shook his head. "Not really. But the minute the crown jewels went missing we started to keep an eye on England's most notorious thieves and safe crackers."

"Mr. Smythe is a notorious safe cracker?" asked Lissy, astonished.

Sergeant Carter shook his head. "Not Smythe. Gary."

"So why were you watching Smythe?" asked Henri.

Inspector Watts took another sip of tea. "Didn't we mention it? Nick and Gary aren't the only two brothers in the Ratcliffe family. There's one more."

"It's Rupert," said Olivia, grinning from ear to ear.

P.C. Pickle almost dropped his chocolate biscuit. "How did you know that?"

Olivia was suddenly shy. "When I was in the graveyard, Rupert was saying words that didn't make sense. When I figured out it was *him* speaking like Billy I asked Aidan to look up certain words in his *Cockney Rhyming Slang* book."

"Well I'll be jiggered," said P.C. Pickle.

"One of the words was manhole cover," said Aidan.

Lissy remembered back to The Tower and the tea and biscuits with Tom and Iris. *What had Iris been trying to teach them about rhyming slang?* "Manhole cover, cover rhymes with—"

"Brother," everyone yelled together.

"Exactly!" said Sergeant Carter. "Rupert Smythe is actually better known as the third Ratcliffe brother – Roger."

"So Roger wasn't imitating a London accent – that *was* his accent," said Aidan. "It was his posh accent that was fake."

Cagney's eyes bulged. "Roger? What kind of name is Roger?"

"I can't believe Gary and Nick are related to Rupert. I mean Roger, I mean ..." Lissy trailed off. "Whatever his name is."

"Roger Ratcliffe!" said Sally, dismissively. "Doesn't have quite the same ring to it as Rupert Smythe, does it?"

"It doesn't!" said Sergeant Carter. "Hence the change of name. Plus they obviously didn't want anyone in the village to know they were brothers. That's why they only spoke on the phone and then once a week in secret in the graveyard."

"We were pretty sure they were involved in this mess," said Inspector Watts. "But we couldn't prove it. Gary disappeared as soon as the jewels went missing. Roger had taken on an alias. And Nick? Well, Nick's always been as crooked as a six-pound note."

"You had your work cut out for you," said Basil. "It's pretty hard to hide someone in a place as small as Bumble Bottom."

"We thought it would be easy to spot Gary if he showed up. But no-one reported anything out of the ordinary," said Sergeant Carter.

"Of course, what we didn't know was Nick had found the perfect hiding space. A hidey-hole laid undiscovered for three-hundred years," said Inspector Watts.

"He must have found it when he fixed up the guest rooms," said Sally. "I've lived in the Googly Gherkin all my life and who'd 'ave thought it? Dick Turpin's hide-out, right above me head."

"It was perfect," said Lissy. "Steal the jewels and hide them until all the fuss died down."

"What the Ratcliffes couldn't reckon on was the police descending on the village just as they were stashing the jewels," said Inspector Watts.

"They couldn't reckon on the plumbing in the castle going out, either," said P.C. Pickle.

"Actually, that's the one thing we can count on, eh, Basil?" said Henri, pouring another cup of tea.

"He was furious when I agreed to put up the Twits said Sally. "Now I know why."

"The only way to reach Gary is through the room Sally gave Olivia and Tess," said Aidan. "Poor Gary must have been starving. Not to mention freezing."

"Rupert wouldn't let his brother leave until he was sure they weren't being watched. So, Nick had been feeding him," said Sergeant Carter.

"Ah," said Sally, "so that's why all that food went missing."

"But when Nick got arrested it was up to his brother to feed Gary," said Inspector Watts.

"And," said Lissy, "when Rupert tried to bring him food ..."

"We interrupted him," said Olivia.

"So that's what he was doing," said Cagney.

"No one goes on a picnic with just one ham sandwich," said Tess. "I could have told you that."

"Yep, poor Gary was stuck in the attic with no food, no light and no heat. He dressed like Dick Turpin not to scare you, but because the clothes he found were warmer than his own," said Inspector Watts.

"So that's who I saw at the end of my bed," said Tess. "I told you Dick Turpin ate my sausage roll."

"I bet Gary heard Lissy talking about how much food Tess had," said Aidan. "He was so hungry, he must have crept out from behind the wardrobe when you guys were asleep."

Olivia shuddered.

Cagney pursed her lips. "But it wasn't Dick Turpin, was it? It was Gary. I don't know how you could be so easily fooled. Puh! I could have told you ghosts don't exist."

Lissy leaned back in her chair. This was no time to fight. This was a time for celebration. The bad guys had been caught and the stolen jewels were tucked away in the Featherington-Twits' safe. All in all, it had been a good day's work.

"Not only did you recover all the jewels stolen from the Tower, but the stash of clothes, coins and trinkets found in Dick Turpin's hideaway is going to make one young lady a very rich woman," said Inspector Watts.

Sally raised her teacup, beaming.

"But I still don't understand how the jewels were stolen in the first place," said Aidan. "Kevin said the Tower was impossible to break in *or* out of."

Major Puffin shifted uncomfortably. His neck, a delicate shade of crimson, flamed upward.

Henri leaned forward and put a hand on Puffin's arm. "You don't have to tell them if you don't want to, Puffin."

"Exactly," echoed Basil. "You weren't to know he was a no-good jewel thief. I mean, I like to think we welcome all sorts to Bumble Bottom, but I think we can safely say, this was a first."

Puffin picked up his teacup and raised it to his lips. "It's going to come out in the long run," he said miserably. "Might as well get it over and done with."

Sergeant Carter took out his notebook. "I'll be asking for a formal statement later, but we might as well get the gist of it."

Puffin sighed, rose to his feet and offered his wrists to the constable. "I plead guilty on all counts."

46

Fooled

Lissy gasped. "Major Puffin is an accomplice?"

Henri grabbed Puffin by the sleeve and yanked him into his chair. "I say, don't be such a drama queen, Puffin. Doesn't suit you at all."

Aidan frowned. "I'm confused. Did Major Puffin just admit to stealing the crown jewels?"

Lord Featherington-Twit rose to his feet. "No, he did not. Stupid man! Do you want to end up in jail with the rest of them, Puffin?"

"Oh, for goodness sake, I'll tell them," said Henri. "All right, Puffin?"

Major Puffin pulled out a red spotted handkerchief and gave his nose a good blow.

"It's quite simple," said Henri. "Puffin was as taken in as the rest of us. When Smythe came to the village he and Puffin struck up an unlikely friendship."

"We had tea every Friday," said Puffin.

"You did indeed," said Henri, patting the old man's arm. "And slowly, Puffin learned to trust Smythe. As we all know, Puffin's a good sort, but he's not exactly the best when it comes to keeping secrets."

Major Puffin shook his head. "I can't believe what a fool I've been."

"Yes, well, can't be helped. You were a fool and you might as well admit it. But you were *not* an accomplice. Now where was I?" asked Henri.

"Tea," said Tess, helpfully.

"Oh yes," said Henri, warming to her topic. "Puffin and Rupert would have tea."

"With chocolate biscuits and buttered scones," interjected Puffin.

"Yes, and during these little tea parties Smythe feigned interest in Puffin's past. I mean really, this should have been your first clue, man. But interest he had, and Puffin opened up like a rose in summer. Told him all about the security system at the

Tower, how he helped build it, how it was installed and, no doubt, what failings it had, if any."

"In my defense, madam, I did not mention I was referring to the Tower's security system."

"Hmpfh!" said Basil. "I suppose you referred to it as a military fortress in the heart of a major city containing national treasures?"

Puffin flushed even redder.

"I expect you did your best, Puffin," said Henri. "Smythe was a charmer, a con-man and you got pulled in with the rest of us."

"A member of the Queen's Regiment should not have been fooled by a two-bit thief, madam."

Sergeant Carter flipped his notebook shut. "I wouldn't exactly call him a two-bit thief, sir. He may not get his hands dirty like his brothers, but he's the brains behind the theft of millions of pounds of treasure."

"He truly is the definition of a master criminal," said Inspector Watts.

"It was his voice that gave the game away," said Olivia. "When he didn't know anyone was listening he spoke just like our friend Billy. There wasn't anyone behind the curtain when we went into Odds and Ends, just Rupert. Same in the graveyard. Both times he was talking on the phone, but in his regular voice. That's what was so confusing."

Inspector Watts nodded. "He would meet Nick every Friday night in the graveyard and tell him what Puffin had told him over tea that day. They even put around a story of the churchyard being haunted, so no one would disturb them."

"I always knew he was up to no good," said Sally. "Just look at him. He was too good looking by half. And, as for that posh voice, well, he didn't have me fooled. Not one little bit."

Puffin clattered his teacup onto the table. "Anyhow, that's about the long and short of it. The reason the Ratcliffe family was able to steal the crown jewels is because they had direct information from the man who set up the entire system - me."

"I'd still like to know who left those costumes for us?" said Aidan. "If it wasn't Sally, then who was it?"

"I told you," said Sally. "I just did what the Featherington-Twits told me to."

"Basil told you we'd left costumes for our American friends to wear?" asked Henri.

"Not to my face," said Sally. "But he called to tell me. Said he'd forgot to mention it and wanted to be sure the cousins got to enter the fancy dress competition."

Basil shook his head. "I think Smythe was better at masking his voice than you give him credit for, Miss Bishop."

Sally looked puzzled.

"Well, if it wasn't Basil who phoned and it wasn't me," said Henri, "I don't think it takes the greatest detective to work out who left the costumes."

"Of course," said Aidan. "It was Rupert. He must have snuck in the back door and left them in the Featherington-Twits' room."

"I *knew* I'd seen those costumes before," said Lissy. "Cagney was looking at them in Odds and Ends the first time we went in. He must have placed the costumes on the Featherington-Twits' bed after we lost sight of him in the cowshed."

"I bet he thought if we were caught up in the fancy dress competition he'd be able to get into the Googly Gherkin and feed Gary," said Aidan.

"What?" said Sally. "No, it was definitely Lord Featherington-Twit. I'd know his voice anywhere."

There was silence.

Sally banged her fist on the table making the teacups dance. "Darn it. I was had."

47

The White Lady

The party continued until night claimed the day. Filled with good cheer, Major Puffin, Sally and the three policemen waved their goodbyes and disappeared over the drawbridge.

"I'm afraid you will be leaving us tomorrow," said Henri, as they headed back into the castle.

"Yep, we'll probably be flying back to the States any day now," said Aidan, sadly.

Basil sighed. "Yes, according to Carrington your grandma just called. Apparently, she visited the palace earlier and personally informed the queen of the recovery. She will be joining us tomorrow and, I'm sorry to say, taking you back to Texas."

Lissy smiled. She would miss the Featherington-Twits and it seemed like they were going to miss them.

Tess glanced up from playing with the Cindy doll Henri had purchased for her as a surprise. "Did she say anything about having tea?"

Basil scratched his head. "I don't think so. Should she have?"

Tess sighed. "Lilibet promised we'd have tea."

Cagney snorted. "You didn't really think that would happen, did you?"

Tess' shoulder sagged. "Yes, I did. And I think Lilibet did too."

"Oh, my dear." Henri placed an arm around Tess' pink fluffy sweater. "The queen is so dreadfully busy. I'm sure she meant what she said at the time, but if you are leaving tomorrow. Well, I don't see any way around it."

"Maybe next time, eh?" said Basil.

"Maybe," muttered Tess.

Olivia poked her nose over the top of the quilt. "Could you quit sulking and come to bed."

"I'm not sulking," said Tess. "I'm thinking."

Olivia rose to her elbows. "I'm going to regret this, but thinking about what?"

"Ghosts," said Tess.

"I thought we'd figured out ghosts weren't real."

"The Gary ghost wasn't real, but what about the White Lady?"

"I'd forgotten about her," said Olivia.

"I hadn't," said Tess, clutching a small woolen blanket. "I've given it a lot of thought and I'm going to stay up and wait for her."

"That should be fun."

"I thought so," said Tess, slipping out the door.

Tess settled herself in the high-back chair at the end of the hallway and prepared to wait. If there was a white lady, she was determined to see her. And besides, from Cagney's description, she sounded pretty. Tess didn't really care for any color other than pink, but a long white dress definitely had its place.

Tess thought back over the past few days. She thought about Rupert, she thought about Potts, she thought about Marla the Magnificent and then, as the clock struck midnight, her head tilted forward and she thought of nothing.

The clock struck one and Tess' eyes flew open. A draft shivered down the passageway and Tess felt the hairs on the back of her neck bristle. The corridor was lit by shafts of moonlight falling through several windows. Tess wasn't scared, but she was puzzled.

Slowly her eyes closed, only to reopen on hearing a noise farther down the hallway. A shadow edged towards her. It was too tall to be Baskerville, too thin to be Carrington. Tess saw a sweep of white out the corner of her eye and pulled the blanket to her nose.

Soundlessly, the white lady glided towards her. Her pale gown swept the floor, her hair, a halo of white, lay upon her shoulders.

Tess stifled the scream welling in her throat. She had come to see the ghost and now she was seeing her. Reaching the bend in the corridor the ghost paused just long enough for the moon to illuminate her spectral face. Tess gasped.

48

Visitor

O livia woke the next day and automatically knew Tess was not there. For one, the sheets were uncrumpled and for two, there was no smell of donuts.

Olivia rolled over and stretched. Slipping from the bed she padded across the room and swung the door wide. She poked her head into the hallway's early morning light and scanned the corridor. The chair sat empty.

Olivia nudged open Cagney and Lissy's door - no Tess. Moving down the corridor she sneaked a peek into Aidan's room - still no Tess. Good grief, the child needed a leash.

Aidan's head poked up from beneath the quilt. The entire left side of his face shone purple. The right side was yellow. "Were you looking for me?"

Olivia shook her head. "Nope, the small Chinese one."

Aidan's smile turned into a wince. "She's slippery."

Olivia sighed. "She's something."

"Give me five and I'll help you search."

The door to Olivia's right creaked opened revealing a disheveled Lissy. "Gone again?"

Olivia nodded.

"Give us a second and we'll come too." Lissy shut the door and Olivia heard her cousin attempt to get Cagney out of bed. Cagney was never her best in the morning. Come to think of it, it was hard to think of a time Cagney *was* her best.

Olivia slipped back into her room to find flip-flops and a sweater. She appeared seconds later to find her three cousins waiting. None of them looked particularly good, but Cagney was, by far, the worse. With a long crease covering one side of her face and her hair standing almost on end, she had definitely looked better. The beige fluffy slippers in the shape of corgis (her prize for winning the fancy dress competition) didn't help much either.

"Come on," said Aidan. "It's our last day in England, we might as well find Tess and make the most of it."

The four traipsed down the wide staircase and stopped.

Lissy wrinkled her nose. "Do you smell something?"

Olivia sniffed. "Follow that smell!"

The four moved silently along the hallway to the back of the castle. Pushing open a door, the aroma wafted over them. Olivia licked her lips.

Tess and Henri stood by the stove piling bacon onto an already heaped plate. From the debris surrounding them, it looked like they'd been there for some time.

"Come in, come in," said Henri. "Tess and I got hungry and decided to do something about it. Anyone fancy a nibble?"

The cousins drew out chairs and plonked themselves around the table. Plates were quickly distributed and the bacon divided with plenty to spare. Heaps of creamy scrambled eggs accompanied it and a tower of toast, dripping with butter, was produced from the oven. The room grew silent as the six devoured the food, until one by one they clattered their cutlery onto empty plates.

"I didn't realize how hungry I was," said Lissy.

Henri rose. She was still in her long white nightgown, her hair, normally prim and proper, flowed down her back. Lissy frowned. There was something about Henri that looked familiar, but what was it?

"So," said Olivia," did you find your ghost?"

Tess smiled. "Not exactly." She grabbed her plate and followed Henri towards the sink.

Lissy couldn't swear to it, but she was sure she saw Henri wink at Tess.

"I didn't know ladies did the dishes," said Cagney, watching Henri pile plates into the sink.

"Ah yes," said Henri, "ghastly, isn't it? But even servants need a day off every once in a while."

Lissy smiled. "Your staff has been so kind. Especially Carrington and the girl with the red hair."

"Oh yes," said Tess. "She's so sweet."

Henri ripped off a rubber glove and turned. "What girl with red hair?"

"You know," said Aidan, blushing. "The pretty one in the old-fashioned dress."

"The one who let us in the other night," said Cagney. "She led me all through the castle. I'd never have found my room without her."

"No one let you into the castle the other night," said Henri. "Basil just left the door ajar."

"But she was there," said Cagney, confused.

"She's always there," agreed Olivia.

The others nodded.

Henri frowned. "I assure you. I'm on first-name terms with all the staff and unless the cook has gone nuts with the food coloring again, there is not a single member of staff that has even remotely red hair."

The lights flickered and a coldness descended upon the room. A shiver went down each cousins' spine as they stared at each other. Nobody said a word.

The cousins were brought back from their thoughts by the jingling of the doorbell. Baskerville, dazed from the vast amount of food dropped from Tess' lap, appeared from under the table and tore along the corridor.

Henri glanced at the clock. "Bit early for visitors, isn't it?"

"I'll get it," said Tess, following Baskerville.

"Go," said Henri. "I'll put the kettle on."

Through a window Aidan could see the familiar Rolls parked beyond the drawbridge. "It's Grandma! James must have driven her here from London."

Lissy smiled. She had so much to tell. Tess reached the door first, but the heavy iron latch was large and stiff.

"Move," commanded Cagney. Quickly, she released the catch and pulled. Cagney's eyes opened wide and for once she didn't say a word.

Tess poked her head around the door and rushed into the arms of her friend. "I knew you'd come! And guess what? You're just in time for tea."

Let's See What You Know

1. In what continent is Great Britain located?
2. Name the four different countries that make up Great Britain.
3. What is the capital of Great Britain?
4. What type of currency do they use in Great Britain?
5. Name the river running through the capital.
6. What is the name of the London suspension bridge that opens and closes?
7. What is St. Stephen's Tower better known as?
8. Who tried to blow up the Houses of Parliament in 1605?
9. What is the name of the current monarch?
10. What are the names of the two British flags mentioned?
11. What is Her Majesty's Royal Palace and Fortress better known as?
12. What is famously housed there?

13. What is the name of the gate that prisoners passed through?

14. What do you call the queen's official bodyguards?

15. Name the famous English king who had six wives?

16. What do you call people born within the sound of Bow Bells?

17. What language do they speak?

18. What is the name of the famous English highwayman?

19. What is the name of the men and women who dance traditional English folk dances?

20. Can you name three royal residencies? (Hint: Major Puffin's corgis)

Answers

1. Great Britain is located in Europe.

2. Great Britain consists of Scotland, Wales, Northern Ireland and England.

3. London is the capital of Great Britain.

4. The British currency is called the pound.

5. The Thames runs through London.

6. The name of the bridge is Tower Bridge.

7. St. Stephen's Tower is more commonly known as Big Ben.

8. Guy Fawkes was the man who tried to blow up the Houses of Parliament.

9. Queen Elizabeth II is the current monarch.

10. The two flags mentioned are the Union Jack and the Royal Standard.

11. Her Majesty's Royal Palace and Fortress is better known as the Tower of London.

12 The Tower of London is the home of the crown jewels.

13. Prisoners passed through Traitor's Gate at the Tower of London.

14. The queen's official bodyguards are called Yeoman Warders or Beefeaters.

15. King Henry VIII is the famous English king who had six wives.

16. People born within the sound of Bow Bells are called Cockneys.

17. Cockneys speak Cockney rhyming slang.

18. The name of the famous British highwayman is Dick Turpin.

19. Men and women who dance traditional folk dances are called Morris Men or Morris Dancers.

20. The three royal residences mentioned in Operation Jewel Thief are Buckingham Palace, Windsor Castle and Balmoral.

Operation Jewel Thief is dedicated
to the following children:

Anyi, now known as Isobel, adopted from Hunan, China on September 18th, 2003

Bao Xin Si, now known as Amy-Li, adopted from Guangdong, China on January 23rd, 2008

Carey-Guo YaYa, now known as Bailee, adopted from Hunan, China on August 8th, 1999

Chen Yazhu, now known as Sara Ann, adopted from Fujian, China on July 9th, 1999

Cheng Qiang, now known as Maggie, adopted from Hubei, China on September 2nd, 2003

Dang Gui Di, now known as Alex, adopted from Shaanxi, China on July 3rd, 2007

Dong Fang Jiangli, now known as Miranda, adopted from Jiangxi, China on August 9th, 2005

Dong Fang Mei, now known as Lily Jing, adopted from Yangdong, China in July 2007

Dong Fang QuLin, now known as Jenai, adopted from Jiangxi, China on August 10th, 2005

Feng Si Hui, now known as Amy, adopted from Jiangxi , China on February 3rd, 2004

Fu Aoyin, now known as Paxton, adopted from Shangdong, China on June 29th, 2015

Fu Hua Li, now known as Emily, adopted from Jiangxi, China on February 1st, 2004

Fu Shana, now known as Lily, adopted from Jiangxi, China on February 1st, 2004

Fu Xiao Jing, now known as Joanna, adopted from Jiangxi, China in February 2004

Fu Xue Zhen, now known as Kelly, adopted from Jiangxi, China on February 1st, 2004

Gan Xin Li, now known as Miah, adopted from Jiangxi, China on July 21st, 2008

Gao Jie Si, now known as Kassidy, adopted from Guangdong, China on July 18th, 2004

Gao Jie Xiao, now known as Isabella, adopted from Guangdong, China on July 18th, 2004

Guo Jing Nong, now known as Ava, adopted from Guangxi, China on June 7th, 2004

Guo Mei Xi, now known as Abigail, adopted from Guangdong, China in December 2001

Guo Wen Ji, now known as Kendall, adopted from Guangxi, China on October 17th, 2003

Guy Chayu, now known as Madelyn, adopted from Jiangxi, China on August 8th, 1999

Huai Chun Xie, now known as Olivia, adopted from Anhui, China on November 1st, 1999

Jiang Ge, now known as Andie, adopted from Chongqing, China

Jiang Mei You, now known as Jacqueline, adopted from Chongqing, China on November 13th, 2006

Jiang Xiao Ting, now known as Julia, adopted from Guangxi, China on March 17th, 2002

Jiang Yuan, now known as Astrid, adopted from Chongqing, China on October 27th, 2003

Jiang Yy Xin, now known as Libby, adopted from Guangdong, China on July 7th, 2001

Jin Mei Yan, now known as Yan Yan, adopted from Guangxi, China on Ocotber 13th, 2009

Jin Rui An, now known as Olivia, adopted from Jiangxi, China on March 17th, 2002

Jin Rui Huan, now known as Delaney, adopted from Jiangxi, China on March 17th, 2002

Jin Rui Qing, now known as Elizabeth, adopted from Jiangxi, China on March 17th, 2002

Jing Ya, now known as Faith, adopted from Shaanxi, China on January 16th, 2006

John, adopted from Texas, USA on March 7th, 2002

Lin Kai Qiao, now known as Millie, adopted from Guangxi, China on November 2nd, 2004

Lin Li Tan, now known as Grace, adopted from Hubei, China on November 11th, 2001

Ling Wu Tao, now known as Allegra, adopted from Jiangxi, China on August 12th, 2007

Liu Yang Bo, now known as Macy, adopted from Guangxi, China on March 20th, 2006

Lou Fu Chin, now known as Victoria, adopted from Hunan, China on October 10th, 2005

Luo Huiqing, now known as Olivia, adopted from Hunan, China on May 12th, 2003

LuXue, adopted from Jiangsu, China on July 16th, 2012

Mamush Bekele, now known as Owen, adopted from Addis Ababa, Ethiopia on March 5th, 2005

Mao Huan Shi, now known as Ruthie, adopted from Guangdong, China on July 18th, 2004

Mi Rou, now known as Maya, adopted from Guangdong, China on November 15th, 2011

Min Xin Yu, now known as Lyric, adopted from Guizhou, China in December 2010

Ping Yun, now known as Tilly, adopted from Guangzhou, China on March 20th, 2006

Po Mei, now known as Mia, adopted from Jiangxi, China on November 28th, 2005

Qi FuJun, now known as Alayna, adopted from Hunan, China on May 15th, 2000

Qi Jia Te, now known as Meisha, adopted from Hubei, China on May 14th, 2007

Qin Xiao Juan, now known as Theresa Lin, adopted from Shaanxi, China on March 25th, 2002

Qing Fu Fan, now known as Andrew (AJ), adopted from Gansu, China on February 6th, 2012

Qing Yi Nan, now known as David, adopted from Gansu, China on February 6th, 2012

Qui Xiao He, now known as Ella, adopted from Guangdong, China on February 9th, 2004

Qui Xin, now known as Quin, adopted from Henan, China on June 9th, 2014

Shangguan Xin Ting, now known as Sam, adopted from Jiangxi, China on January 18th, 2010

She Chen, now known as Catherine, adopted from Hunan, China on November 10th, 2003

Shen Chunying, now known as Anna Nicole, adopted from Zhejiang, China on November 1st, 1996

Sui Xiao Pei, now known as Abby, adopted from Guangdong, China on February 2nd, 2004

Tang Liang, now known as Lena, adopted from Zhejiang, China on January 4th, 2002

Wan Jin Fu, now known as Jordan, adopted from Jiangxi, China on June 17th, 2001

Wu JiaYan, now known as Miami, adopted from Hebei, China on April 13th 2015

William, adopted from Florida, USA on January 18th, 2011

Xiao Fu, now known as Lauren, adopted from Guangxi, China on March 17th, 2002

Xiao Lian, now known as Claire, adopted from Hunan, China

Xiaoxue, now known as Maya, adopted from Jiangxi, China on February 1st, 2004

Xie Xie, now known as Lily, adopted from Jiangxi, China on March 17th, 2002

Xin Hao Min, now known as Lily, adopted from Guangxi, China on July 1st, 2004

Yan Jia Huai, now known as Sophie, adopted from Hunan, China on December 1st, 2009

Yang Hua Yin, now known as Paulina, adopted from Guangdong, China on June 2nd, 2013

Yang Li, now known as Rachel, adopted from Hunan, China on September 16th, 2002

Yang Long Yuan, now known as Corbin, adopted from Hunan, China on June 30th, 2015

Yangxi Zi Yu, now known as Daisy, adopted from Guangdong, China on June 19th, 2007

Ye Gan Qun, now known as Aubrey, adopted from Zhejiang, China

Ye Meng Lei, now known as Lian, adopted from Hubei, China on August 14th, 2006

Yi Ke Fang, now known as Kaitlyn, adopted from Jiangxi, China on December 2nd, 2007

Yi Li Jing, now known as Rachel, adopted from Jiangxi, China on February 1st, 2004

Yi Li Dan, now known as Maia, adopted from Jiangxi, China on November 14th, 2002

Yi Li Wei, now known as Tess, adopted from Jiangxi, China on February 1st, 2004

Yi Li Xu, now known as Natalie, adopted from Jiangxi, China on February 1st, 2004

Yong Lanye, now known as Gabrielle, adopted from Hunan, China on July 11th, 2005

Yue Yu Hao, now known as Maria, adopted from Jiangxi, China on November 20th, 2005

Zhao Kai Xin, now known as Kai, adopted from Henan, China on October 21st, 2014

Zhi Yao, now known as Lauren, adopted from Hunan, China on May 28th, 2007

Zhu Fu Mei, now known as Katelyn, adopted from Guangdong, China on January 3rd, 2006

And my sweet friend, Jess, wonderful big sister to Emily and Kate.

Book Discussion Points

The air stewards have very distinct accents that the cousins find hard to understand. Have you ever met someone hard to communicate with? How did you overcome this?

During the book Tess keeps disappearing and worrying her cousins. Have you ever done anything to make your family worried and if so did you learn a lesson?

The cousins take part in a fancy dress competition. What costume would best represent you?

Lissy realizes she's been wearing a tea-cosy as a hat. Have you ever done anything embarrassing? What was your reaction?

Do you believe in ghosts?

What countries would you like to visit?

Which cousin is your favorite and why?

Acknowledgments

England was an utter joy to write. My thanks go to the following for making it possible.

Firstly, author and critique partner, Lindsey Scheibe, who has encouraged me from the start. And sadly, for the last time, I thank our partner in crime – the talented and hugely missed, Raynbow Gignilliat.

I am also thankful to the amazing Han Randhawa who continues to outdo himself with his beautiful cover art. It is a joy to collaborate with such immense talent.

For offering to post bail money as I questioned Yeomans on how to steal the queen's jewels, I thank Mumpsy and my girls, who drive patiently around my beloved England with me each summer.

Melissa Fong, who not only beta reads all my books, but helps organize and direct me – not an easy feat!

Stephanie Hudnall for being my go-to person for practically everything and always answering my unending questions with a smile.

Samantha Clark and Chris Eboch for their mad editing skills.

First readers Claire Fahey, Kathleen Murphy Laura and Jane Grovers, , Cara Beth and MacKenzie McLeod – thank you all, especially those of you who said it was your favorite book.

My friends at Westbank Community Library, whose continued support is so appreciated.

Fellow authors, Karen MacInerney, whose mysteries encourage me to be a better and funnier writer and Erin Edwards for encouragement and delicious, tax deductible Greek lunches.

Olivia's adored third grade teacher, Karly Taylor Cummins, for her contribution to this book in the form of prickly pear cactus jelly!

Macy!

And finally, to the children on whose these characters are based. We are beyond blessed to have such kind and wonderful cousins in our lives.

ABOUT THE AUTHOR

Photo by Dave Wilson

Sam Bond was born in London, raised in
Shropshire and has lived all over the world. She
currently lives in Austin, TX with two of the five
cousins. *Operation Jewel Thief* is the third book in the
Cousins In Action series.

You can find Sam online at:
www.5cousinsadventures.com.
Or on Facebook at 5 Cousins Adventures

Read more adventures in the first two Cousins In Action books: Operation Golden Llama and Operation Tiger Paw and join the cousins on their next journey to the wild deserts of Egypt. Explore this magical kingdom as the cousins come face to face with crocodiles and camels, pyramids and pharaohs, ancient tombs and mummies, all while trying to avoid getting cursed!

Made in the USA
Middletown, DE
15 February 2016